THE LOST TOMES OF ZENAFROST

VOLUME ONE

THE BORNBANE SERIES

I.A. TAKERIAN

This is a work of fiction. The characters, incidents, and dialogues are products of the author's imagination and are not to be construed as real. Any resemblance to actual events or persons, living or dead, is entirely coincidental.

Cover Art by Moonpress.com

Chapter headings drawn by Etheric Tales

Created with Vellum

THE LOST TOMES OF ZENAFROST

VOLUME ONE

I. A. TAKERIAN

CHAOS MAGICK

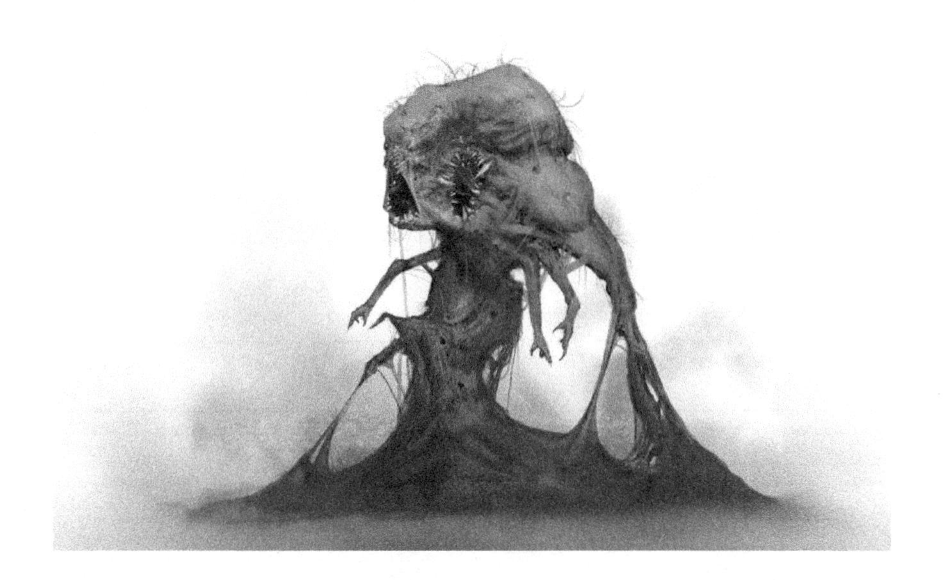

DARKLING

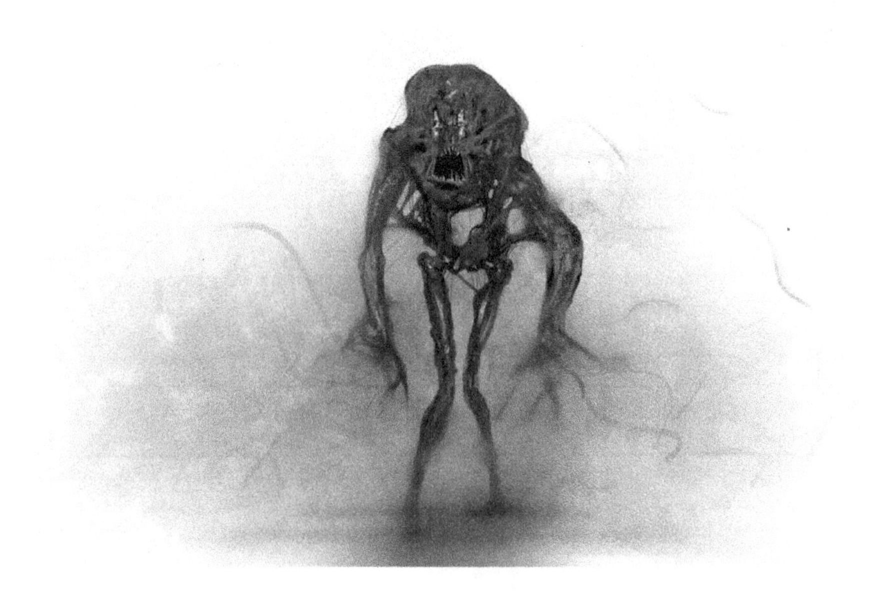

REFLECTOR BEAST

THE NECROMANCER

In the Seventh Era, during the events of the Druidic Wars, many ancient artifacts were unearthed by the explosion of battle. Among these was the Library of the Eldest.
Previously thought lost to time, the library contained innumerous texts and tomes dating all the way back to the very birth of Zenafrost. Many of these are still in the process of refurbishment, but a select few have been deciphered and transcribed into the following pages.

Attention: As Decreed By Our Great King Lionas Dawnbringer In The Seventh Era Of The Sun.

THIS BOOK IS NOT TO BE REMOVED FROM THE GREAT HALL LIBRARY FOR ANY REASON, OTHER THAN BY ORDER OF THE KING OR QUEEN RESIDING.
LONG LIVE THE DAWNBRINGER.

INTRODUCTION

In the beginning of all, there were the Zenoths. Beings born of pure stardust and the natural stream of magick that flows through the cosmos. They were beautiful, mighty, formidable. They held the power to create entire worlds by their hand, lush with green hills and rolling seas.
But none alone held the magick powerful enough to birth sentient life onto these great worlds.
This was a lonely existence for beings who felt their sole purpose was to render that vital spark. Many yearned to share their overflowing love with those other than themselves. To use their wonderous powers for something greater. Thus, the assembly was called, gathering the Zenoths together for the first time in a millennium to discuss the possibility of a new age...

CHAPTER 1
THE OPENING OF THE COSMOS

The light was blinding, a million fractured rainbows fighting for their place in the dew-speckled air. Splendor beyond measure in every way, though it always was in the Chamber of the Sun. Axoliphim stepped from the rift he had travelled in through, squinting hard against the sudden brightness. His thick ebony curls fell about his shoulders, shielding his eyes like two vibrant rays of moonlight through the dark shroud. He grimaced. This was a far cry from the Library of Everlast, the place he had spent the last three hundred years of his existence. Already, he longed to be back between the spiraling shelves, floating amongst the books as he absorbed every ounce of knowledge that ever was or will be.

But his eldest sister had called this gathering. And that meant something far too important to miss.

Ax waved his hand, conjuring a purple cloud below his feet that he promptly perched upon. It began to rise through the sun-bleached landscape, lifting him high into the air. His destination lay some ways above him: a massive, dazzling crystal, rotating slowly in the ether. Pieces of fallen stars and planetary dust spun circles around it, stuck in eternal orbit. He could see the silhouettes of his siblings already gathered here, and a slight frown came to his face.

They were all in their true forms, brilliant and handsome even from this distance. Threads of constellations whispered off their skin, each a different hue of light and dark. Many wore cloaks and robes of the finest make, donning crowns wrought of moonbeams and softly pulsing jewels.

Some were fully clothed, others starkly naked as they hovered on their respective clouds. Ax, in contrast, was in his customary Librarian robes. Dull fabric in shades of orange, green and purple that he had spun himself. Shimmering gold thread made scrolling designs across the chest, but they paled in comparison to the attire surrounding him.

Ax felt the eyes of his siblings on him as he joined their circle. They had never approved of him, overall, and it had been well over a hundred years since last he attended the Chamber. From his decision to remain in the Library of Everlast instead of building worlds like the rest, to his starkly distant personality...his family loved him, but Ax was aware of his status amongst most of the group.

A Zenoth was rising to hover above the giant crystal in the center of their gathering. The tallest of them, and by far the most stunning. She wore white cloaks made of what looked like liquid sunbeams, floating around her in a hypnotic dance. She had no hair, but an ornate crown made of living flowers sprouted from her midnight black skin. There was a thin cloth draped from her forehead, shimmering like rainfall as it shadowed her eyes. Ax gave a sigh of admiration and reverence, as he always did when his sister rose to speak.

Diminora, or Nora, as Ax had always called her, was the very first Zenoth to be born from the cosmos. She had welcomed them into the world, taught each of them to use their magicks; to harness their powers and pour them into creating good in the universe. Her soul was the utmost pure, her heart wanting only to *give, give, give*. And it was this unconditional love that made them all bow before her eternal glory.

A hush fell over the Zenoths as she raised her hands high, a smile brimming on her perfect face. “My blood! My kin! I welcome you home, back into the warmth of the Chamber. It was here we were born, here our purpose began.” She spun slowly, revolving to face each of them in turn. When her eyes met Ax, he blushed and offered a bashful smile.

Nora had never judged Ax, never made him feel lesser for his differences or indecisions. It was true, this Chamber is where they had been brought in to being, one by one. But it was Nora that Ax called ‘home.’

She waved a hand behind her, and a man made of glimmering starlight stepped forth. Their brother, Bardro, was older by far than Ax. His skin, wrought of cosmic dust and etched in ancient symbols, glistened in the glow from the crystal. Long white hair furled out from the hood of a nearly invisible cloak, like tendrils of snow against the sun-soaked air.

Bardro was the reason Ax had devoted the brunt of his own life to knowledge, and the secrets the world held. His elder brother was an alchemist, a philosopher, a magician; a mixer of many different lost arts into one mighty power. Ax had plenty a fond memory of sitting atop his shoulders as a child, watching him read once-vanished tomes and solve the mysteries of thousands of worlds.

Bardro lowered the hood of his cloak, revealing his pristine face. Ax had not seen him for many moons now, and he studied the new, scrolling etches of runes carved deep in his brother’s cheeks. No doubt done by his own hand, as Ax had seen him do to most all the others across his body.

His ice blue eyes gazed out across the Zenoths, as appraising as they had ever been.

“As you all know, I have devoted these last lightyears to the study of the soul. To what it truly means. Not just the study, but the implication. The *application*.”

There was silence at his words.

It was well known to all Zenoths that Nora had been trying to create sentient life since before any of them even existed. And though she struggled endlessly, pouring every ounce of herself in to this one dream, none ever came. The power it took to create a soul was too much for even the great Zenoths to achieve.

Ax knew how much it broke Nora's heart, being incapable of the thing she so yearned for. It only made sense that she would enlist Bardro's assistance in this task, though Ax felt a small pang of jealousy that she had never thought to ask *him*. Bardro was speaking again, pulling Ax from his brooding.

"It is my greatest honor to stand before you now, in this most sacred place, finally successful in this endeavor." Nora and Bardro each raised a hand, placing them side by side on the crystal's glassy surface. A shared vision, clear as the Chamber around them, glowed forth and overtook each Zenoth.

In the vision, they all stood together, somewhere high above the Chamber of the Sun. All of Ax's brothers and sisters, hovering in the great blackness of the cosmos and channeling their magicks into one, brilliant ball of light. They began to chant in the ancient tongue, and as they did so, the glowing light became impossibly bright. The chant seemed to reach its climax, there was a mighty ***bang***, and the vision came to an abrupt halt.

Whispers began at once.

"That looked like an *ending* of life, Nora. Not a beginning," Ax's sister, Friya, said in a very soft voice.

"No one has ever accomplished such a thing. Not in all the passings of the planets or the Beyonds. What makes you think this time would be any different?" His brother, Yvor, said on the other side of him with a heavy frown.

"Joining our magicks like that...it could have cataclysmic consequences, brother. You know this," Readan said, stroking his beard thoughtfully.

"Now, now."

A deep voice cut across the anxious whispers, silencing them in an instant. Another man was joining Nora and Bardro at the center of the Chamber. The second Zenoth born to the universe, Mezilmoth. His robes were wrought of smoke and moonlight, laced together with the remnants of some far-off planet he had surely once created. His step was sure, his eyes soft as he bowed his head respectfully at Nora. He folded his hands neatly before him, his silver hair like star-strewn rope across his left shoulder.

"Brothers, sisters, soullings. We were granted sentience and power from the cosmos for the sole purpose of evolution. Not only the evolution of ourselves, but of our universe. It is the gift, and the duty, that was bestowed upon us by the stars." He smiled, turning his violet eyes skyward and watching their fraction of universe fly past above the stationary Chamber. "We would be doing this purpose a great disservice, were we to not at least attempt this next, mighty leap into the unknown. A life without change, a life without *knowledge*...that is no life at all, my kin. Do you not agree?"

Ax sat up straighter, eyes alight. He could see the same bright look on the faces of his siblings, each now contemplating the possibility of something beautiful and new. This was a gift Mezilmoth had always possessed. A unique skill that made all those who listened to him be swayed by his words. And rightfully so. Ax could not recall a single moment in his life where Mezilmoth's sage advice in these council meetings had been ill-given or taken.

Nora gave a small smile to Mezilmoth, turning back to face the Chamber with arms held wide, "I implore you all to listen. I cannot, *will* not force your heart, but I can share with you what is in mine. And it is overflowing with love, always. A love I yearn so desperately to share with new life, new joy, new *hope.* But I cannot do so without each of you. Please. Let us create a new home *together.* One fit for us *all.*"

Bardro stood tall at Nora's side, head held high as he addressed the Chamber once more, "Who will take up this mantle of creation with us?!"

Ax was on his feet a split second before everyone else. He would have stood by Nora's side, even without the wise words of his brothers. He strode across to the center of the Chamber, Nora beaming down at him as he joined the gathered Zenoths around the great crystal. The buzz of chatter grew as Bardro conjured a massive cloud of energy underfoot, jettisoning them all upwards into the cosmos.

Nora wrapped her powerful arms around Ax's body, pulling him into her warm embrace. "I have missed you so, my brother," she murmured into the top of his head, ruffling the hair, and sending a wave of goosebumps down his spine.

He leaned into her chest, savoring the smell of happiness that seeped from it. "You know me, Nora. Never satisfied unless my brain is constantly fed." He tightened his grip on her as he went on, "But I've missed you miserably as well."

She released him from the hug, sliding her hand into his as they made a tight circle. Ax could see excitement and wonder dancing in the eyes of many of his siblings, fear and uncertainty in the looks of others. But hand in hand they stood nonetheless, just as they had in the vision moments before. The Chamber of the Sun was too far below them to see now, the circle of Zenoths flying along in the steady stream of the Universe. Ax watched constellations whiz past, felt the soft, damp tingle of stardust as it trailed by his cheek.

The cloud ceased rising, dissipating to leave them suspended amongst the stars. All eyes turned now to Bardro, waiting. His brow was set in confident determination, but Ax could tell from the tight line of his lips that he did not know precisely *what* could come of this. His gaze flickered to Nora's for a moment, and courage returned to his presence.

He took a deep breath, one that was mirrored by his siblings, "Clear yourselves. Make your mind a vessel, your heart a pyre. Just as you do to create your own worlds. Focus your intent on the center of our circle. Repeat after me."

And he began to chant. It was in a language Ax recognized, but only barely. Some strange combination of the ancient tongues, magick lilts and an overarching tone that was nearly musical in nature. It was a sound echoed in an instant by the Zenoths. The noise was magnificent, and Ax knew at once that this was something they could not stop even if they wanted to.

As they chanted, a sudden harmonious chiming rose to join their unifying voices. A feeling of immense elation was crashing over Ax, rooting him to the spot beside Nora as a dim glow began at the center of their circle. It was faint, almost impossible to see at first. It pulsed with the cadence of a heartbeat, vein-like streams of light beginning to stretch forth from its core. The glow grew brighter with each passing verse of their chant, the roots of light now seeping into the bodies of the Zenoths. It felt warm, like sun directly through his soul as the light became one with him. It connected each to the glowing orb, and as it attached to the final of Ax's siblings, it suddenly changed.

The pulsing light became a solid mass of incredible energy. This was magick beyond comprehension, beyond anything created before. It took the breath from Ax as the power swept through them all, but they tightened their holds on each other and kept the circle whole. The orb had begun spinning rapidly, faster and faster, sparking with every color imaginable as it picked up speed.

The chant reached a fever-pitch, the voices and melodic chiming now deafening as it shot through the stars. Then there was a world-shattering ***boom***.

White light, pleasure and pain and everything in between, slammed into the Zenoths. It threw them all back through the stars in every direction, rocketing along blindly as an enormous shock-wave of magick collided with their bodies again and again. Ax felt as if he was being ripped apart, destroyed, and reborn in that endless moment of pure nothingness.

The waves of energy subsided, the all-encompassing light dimming. Ax shook his head, ears ringing, steadying himself as he tried to get his bearings. He had fallen amongst a cluster of young stars, displacing them from their constellations. One of the natural streams of magick that ran through the cosmos was feet away and gave an angry quake. Tendrils of power began gathering the stars back to their rightful places. "Sorry," Ax muttered to it over his shoulder, distracted as he peered into the distance.

Far in the sparkling further, somewhere high above the Chamber of the Sun, a new planet had appeared. It was an unbelievable shade of blue, covered almost entirely in crystalline water. But as Ax flew towards it, he began to make out a large continent, lush with green earth. His siblings were gathering on the ground, standing amongst hilly terrain as they surveyed their work. Ax's feet touched the soft grass, and he let out a gasp.

The energy here was different from anything he had ever felt, in all his travels, in all his studies. There was a magick pulse emanating from down below, it felt nearly life-like. This was something...something *new*. It made him feel strangely light, as if every moment in eternity had narrowed down to this very second. He could see this emotion mirrored in his siblings' faces, eyes shining with awe at this incredible place. But it was Nora who Ax's gaze fell instantly on.

This world was a marvel, something too stunning to put into words with its still-growing nature and massive power. It was sure to be filled with mystery and magick; knowledge beyond measure that Ax would be the first to uncover. Nora, however, was staring around with growing disappointment. Her eyes scanned the edge of the dense forest before them, the beautiful smile falling slowly from her face as her searching was met with nothing.

"What incredible power," Mezilmoth was saying softly behind Ax, knelt on the ground with his hands flat against the dirt. His eyes looked hungry, almost wild with whatever he sensed below the surface. He breathed a laugh. "It's like nothing I've ever felt."

"But did it work...?" one of Ax's brothers asked as they studied a nearby tree that was sprouting stunning purple flowers as they watched.

"Shh!" Bardro said with urgency, silencing them all as he stared into the wood. "I can hear something."

He was right, something *was* approaching from the darkness of the tree cover. Branches snapped underneath trembling steps, leaves shifting restlessly as a figure emerged slowly into the light.

It looked like a miniature Zenoth, though muted in color and frail in form. It walked upright on two legs, blonde hair shimmering across her shoulders and curtaining two long, pointed ears. Her eyes looked like flecks of starlight; her tan face gorgeous even in its fear. She shook as she stumbled to a halt, shading her eyes from the sun.

The Zenoths were frozen. Not a single breath was taken as they stared at this new creature, at this new *life*. And it was Ax, always so quiet and withdrawn, that took the first step towards her.

It was a force he couldn't understand that led his feet, a string tethering him closer and closer to the woman from the woods. He held his hand out before him, reminded of how Nora had welcomed him so gently into the universe at his own birth. He remembered how terrifying it was, being thrust from nothing into the sudden 'all' of life. Overwhelming, cold, harsh...it was important to take those feelings from her. For her to know she was safe. The female took a step back, staring at Ax's mighty hand in confusion and fear. And he heard Nora's voice in his memory, the first words he heard in the whole of his existence.

"Be not afraid, starling," he repeated them to her in the gentlest voice as he took another step forward. She was stunning, this child born of magick, glorious and incredible and fragile. *So* fragile. Ax was overcome by a sudden need to protect her, to protect any that came with or after her. This kind of overwhelming love was something he had never felt before.

"Welcome to your life," he cooed to her. "Welcome to the universe, to the cosmos and Beyonds. We've been waiting for you, you know." He extended his hand to her once more, tilting his head as he offered a warm smile.

She stared at the expression for a moment, her gaze darting across his wide grin and back to his kind eyes. And then she did something that took his breath away. Her handsome face shifted into a magnificent, beaming smile. She took Ax's hand, and he felt he would never feel something more delicate again in all his years.

The Zenoths were shaking themselves from their stunned stupor on the hillside as Ax began to walk towards them with the female. Tears were now streaming from Nora's eyes, dashing past her smile, and springing colored flowers of glowing light to life on the grass where they fell. The Zenoths began dancing in unbridled celebration, turning to the female with welcoming arms. Ax felt her hesitate beside him.

He squeezed the female's hand reassuringly as his siblings rushed to them. She turned her incredible eyes back on him, and the trust they held made his smile grow even wider. "Come, little one. There is more of our family out there, new as you. Let us find them together."

Many years have passed since the creation of Zenafrost. The land flourishes, growing and changing with every moment, breathing new life into the world. The beings created by the Zenoth's magick were named the Fae, and they thrived harmoniously in their new home. Each had a place, a drive, a dream.

All was well and right in their corner of the cosmos. The Zenoths loved the Fae so deeply, that they wished to bless them with a gift beyond all others, beyond even the greatest of riches. A celebration was to be held, one which would change the fabric of destiny forever...

CHAPTER 2
STRANGE MAGICK

The Library of Time was one of Ax's greatest achievements to date. A mass of knowledge and wisdom that rivaled even the most extensive in existence; it had taken himself and several of his sibling's years to build its trove. But it was more than worth it to have this stronghold to study Zenafrost.

Most of the Zenoths had been shocked by Ax's decision to stay, so used to his usual solitary lifestyle that they couldn't believe the sudden change. The only ones that truly seemed to understand his reasons for remaining were Nora, Bardro and Mezilmoth. Nora saw the love in his eyes when he looked at the Fae, when he examined the ever-changing landscapes they had created together. Bardro and Mezilmoth each respected his utter need for knowledge, having felt the mighty pull of it themselves. Ax had seen neither of his brothers in months, both gone on their own expeditions into the far reaches of the land. And though he still spent a large portion of his time studying all he could about Zenafrost from the confines of his library, Ax was no longer alone.

He had developed a strong, unbreakable connection with the first Fae they had encountered on this world. The woman from the woods, who had taken the name Velisa. It was impossible to tell how much time had passed since the Fae's creation, as they seemed to be immortal like the Zenoths. Ax had lost count of the months, the years...it felt like he had known Velisa for eternity, unable to recall what life was like before her presence.

Like Ax, she had developed a keen interest in the mysteries of Zenafrost. Since the day of her creation, she had spent barely a moment away from his side. She was an incredible mind, well beyond what one would deem a quick study. Together, they would make grand voyages out into the stunning landscapes, going on adventures that Ax had only ever read about before her. She would often grow restless upon their return to the Library, Ax insisting that he needed time to study their finds and decompress his mind. And now was exactly one of those times.

Ax sat at one of his desks, brow furrowed over his eyes as he studied the plant in his hands. It was pulsating with light and the same strange magicks that emanated from the very core of Zenafrost. Like a steady heartbeat, it made his hand feel almost electrified with power. Velisa was hovering a short way away, poking at a crystal grid that lay across the desk opposite him. Her eyes widened with child-like delight as each sang a different note on contact.

Ax sighed, placing the glowing flower down on the stone desktop and turned to face her, eyebrow raised. "Is there *truly* nothing more productive you could be doing with your time, Vel? Scrolls that need organizing? Tomes that need tending? Herbs that must be pruned?"

Velisa gave a huff of exasperation, dropping dramatically on to the stool by Ax's chair. "I've done all that already and you know it! Can't we join the festivities early like everyone else?"

A wicked smirk played on Ax's face, eyes flashing.

"So eager today. And I suppose it would have nothing to do with Ingard arriving there early himself then?" Ingard was a strong and kind male who had helped to build many of the villages across Zenafrost. Nora often enlisted his help to teach their growing population how to hunt, gather, and craft. Ax had seen the love grow in

Velisa's eyes for him over many years, whenever the two were brought together.

Color rose instantly to her cheeks, her hand lashing out to hit Ax on the leg as he laughed. She looked scandalized, as she always did when he had the gall to mention her obvious feelings. "Oh, bite your tongue! I simply find his prowess with a blade to be quite...*exhilarating.*"

"Ah, is that what you're calling it now?"

Another slap, this time harder as his laughing doubled at her reaction. "***As I was saying,*** I'd like to join the others before the celebration begins. It's so rare a thing for us all to gather these days. I think it's important to soak it in as much as we can." She shuffled anxiously for a moment, her brilliant eyes staring up at Ax through her lashes, "Don't you?"

Ax was reminded again of a child, looking for approval for something they thought might be taken as foolish. She often had this effect on him, warming him to the core. He softened at once, patting her head gently and offering a hearty smile. "I'm only teasing you, starling. You're right, of course."

Velisa was already on her feet, practically leaping with joy. "I nearly always am. Haven't you noticed?"

Ax laughed the hardest yet at this, allowing her to yank him up from his chair. "Let's be off, before you set the whole damned Library ablaze with your madness."

It had been a *great* many years since last Ax saw most of the Fae and his siblings alike. The Fae he had known since the beginning were worlds wiser now, though their eternally perfect faces gave no sign of aging. To his great surprise and utmost joy, there were *children* running through the flower-soaked fields where the celebration was being held. The Fae had begun creating life of their own, populating their gorgeous home with even more beauty.

Velisa and Ax had arrived before the sun set over the mountains. Velisa had vanished from Ax's side at once, appearing almost as quickly at Ingard's shoulder. He had smiled bashfully at her; Velisa returned the look in kind. Ax had given a hearty chuckle, filled a tankard full of sweet valley wine and taken off through the growing crowd in search of Nora.

He stood beside her now in the light from the full moon, drinking and watching the Zenoths and Fae dance, laugh, and sing through the meadows. Nora was as effervescent as ever, adorned in robes that had clearly been made by Fae hands. Dark green, and spun together with delicate silver thread, it was stunning against her glowing black skin. She was beaming at a group of Fae younglings closest to them, staring up at the star-strewn sky as they spun round and round. They were falling to the grass one by one, dizzy and overtaken with giggles. Nora was gazing at them with such love, Ax felt almost breathless in the presence of it.

"I hope you've saved enough of that wine for me, brother," The voice so suddenly near him made Ax jump, spinning in place. Bardro had snuck up behind them, smirking at Ax's surprise. His cloak was dusty, clearly fresh from travel. Ax embraced him, Nora following suit.

"We didn't think you'd make it!" she said, stepping back to appraise his worn appearance. "I've not heard from you for months. Were you traveling the stars?"

Bardro often stole away to other planets, too restless to stay put for long. But he shook his head, taking the filled tankard from Ax's hand. "I've been mapping the continent. Studying its beasts, living amongst its good peoples. Even took on an apprentice from up North near the frosts." He raised his tankard, motioning to a tall Fae man with cropped silver hair. He was talking animatedly to a group of very attentive women. "Name's Kivion. Mind sharp as a dagger, with a tongue to match. He's been assisting me with my studies."

Ax raised an eyebrow as Bardro took a swig of his drink. Nora gave him a look as well, both catching the odd tone in his voice. "And what exactly have you been studying these last years, brother?" Ax asked, curious if he had discovered something Velisa and himself had yet to find.

Bardro lowered the tankard, glancing to make sure they were free of overeager listeners. "I've been trying to figure out the source of the strange magick. We can all feel it, have since we made this place. It's...it's almost overwhelming at times. Constantly underfoot, and all around. If I can pinpoint the heart of it, I might finally be able to understand its mysteries."

Ax nodded at this, thinking of his own research. "It is odd. I've never seen a place that's evolved so rapidly. Every expedition, we seem to bring back new plant and wildlife that have popped up. Not to mention the exponential growth of the land itself."

Nora frowned. "You know, even if you never fully understand this place, it doesn't make it any less beautiful. You can enjoy a thing without needing to pick it apart. The two of you are as bad as Mezilmoth sometimes."

"Yes, where is our dear second in command?" Bardro asked, staring out across the meadows, now rolling with the strange multicolored orb lights that often sprung forth from the ground. "I'd love to pick his brain about what he's seen on his travels."

"I thought *you'd* know where he is," Nora replied, only partially listening as she conjured tiny, iridescent bubbles to flit through the crowd of Fae and Zenoth. Ax watched as they popped into bursts of sparkling stardust, dazzling the merrymakers as they went.

"I've not heard from him in months. Last we spoke, he was on his way to explore the lands in the west," Bardro replied.

Ax gave a sigh, disappointed that he'd miss seeing his eldest brother once again. "It's not the first time he's gotten lost in his studies, and rest assured it won't be the last. You know how devoted he is to his work."

Nora nodded, the smile returning to her face as her eyes sparked with excitement. "Well, I suppose we're all here, if that's the case.

Ingard, dear!" She called out to the place where Ingard and Velisa stood nearly nose to nose, giggling over their drinks. "Will you and Velisa gather the others? I'd say you've all waited long enough for your gifts."

~

THE ZENOTHS and Fae stood gathered round the place where Nora stood. With the full moon poised so perfectly above her, Ax was reminded irresistibly of their gatherings in the Chamber of the Sun. Though none of those came close to the sort of joyous celebration they were all part of here. The Fae were buzzing with excitement and anticipation, the Zenoths amongst them watching with looks of love and fascination.

Nora's smile had yet to come off her face, pinned in what could have been an eternal look of happiness. Silence fell as she raised her hands and spoke. "My family!" she called, her beautiful voice echoing out across the meadows. "These many years have been ones of great prosperity, of jubilation and glee! It is a love the likes of which I have never known, and one I know not how to repay."

All eyes were set on Nora, glistening and bright. "We share this love, share this *home,* as one. I view each of you, Fae and fellow Zenoth alike, as my kin. My equals. And I find it fitting, therefore, that our gift unto you should only serve to deepen that bond."

She motioned towards herself, and the Zenoths stepped forward from the crowd to join her at the center. Ax could feel the excitement, like a buzz of electricity through the air. He himself was bobbing on the balls of his feet, gaze scanning across the wide-eyed faces of the Fae. Velisa was stood beside Ingard, looped to one of his arms while a young girl who looked to be his sister clung to the other. She was staring at Nora with mouth slightly agape, her eyes sparkling as they always did when she was excited.

Nora nodded to Bardro, who took a step forward and addressed the crowd next. "As many of you know, our magicks stem from a core inside each of us. A Zenoth is born from this core, no two exactly alike, each as powerful and magnificent as the last."

He paused here for dramatic effect, a mischievous grin lighting his handsome face as he watched the Fae react to his words. Ax rolled his eyes at his brother's theatrics, stifling a chuckle as he went on. "This magick has opened entire worlds for us; allowed us to create Zenafrost and the beauty that surrounds me now. I see this magick when I look at you all, sparking behind your eyes, hidden in your laughter. And it is this magick that we wish to gift you in earnest."

A hush fell over the crowd. "We wish to bless you all with that which we have been blessed with. To truly set ourselves as equals in the cosmos and begin a new age as *one*. With the alignment of the moon beneath the Chamber of the Sun, each Zenoth can reach into themselves. We can touch that core of magick that resides at our hearts and draw from it two smaller cores. It is these cores we wish to then give to you."

Ax heard Velisa's gasp over all the rest, her eyes instantly flying to his as her hands covered her mouth. He could see tears glittering in her eyes, a look mirrored by many of the Fae. He beamed back at her, feeling tears welling within him as well. This was a dream he knew Velisa held above all others. To wield magick as Ax and the others did; to experience all that eternity had to offer.

Nora raised her hands once more, quieting the excited chatter that had swept across the crowds. "What we speak of is something that has never been done before, never once been attempted in the history of the cosmos. These cores, once split from ourselves, will search for the soul that it is compatible with. Magick can only reside within bodies who are both apt and willing for it, so please: do not feel that you *must* accept this gift. The unknown can be frightening, as can the concept of this power."

Ax watched many of the Fae take gracious steps back from the circled crowd as she said this. They looked relieved, and Nora nodded reassuringly at them. "Magick or no magick, it does not change the might and glory that is each of you."

"Is it going to hurt?!" The tiny voice came from Ingard's sister, still clung to his massive arm and looking frightened. Ingard and Velisa both knelt beside her, comforting her as she stared with wide eyes at Nora.

Nora's beautiful face softened even further, crossing over to the three of them and kneeling before the girl. She held out her hands, smiling like a mother to her child. "I promise you, there will be no pain, Haziel. Only warmth and light. You have nothing to fear."

Haziel hesitated for a moment. Then she pulled herself from Ingard and took Nora's hands, returning her smile with one of her own. Ax felt his heart leap in his chest at the wonder in her eyes; the trust in them. Nora swept her up into her arms, cradling her into her bosom as she returned to her place at the center of the crowd.

"None of you need fear this gift! The magick will only come to those who are able and ready to harness it. It is not a forced thing, but rather a homecoming." She looked down into the now eager face of Haziel, held gently in her arms. "Shall you be the brave soul to go first, my starling?"

Haziel placed a tiny hand on the side of Nora's face, closing her eyes and leaning forward until their foreheads touched. Ax was suddenly struck by an overwhelming need to weep. This was love, pure and true; everything Nora had ever dreamed of or wanted. These people were their family, and this final gift was one that was fate-altering. Ax could feel it in the air: this was destiny.

As Haziel embraced her, Nora placed her spare hand over her own heart. There was a mighty hum, and an energy swept across the meadows. It seemed to swirl around them, growing in power as they stood and watched. Nora's chest was glowing beneath her hand, the color and magnitude of the sun. Ax felt the air shift, as if growing still in the presence of the thing unfolding within it. Nora was pulling her hand from her chest, and with it came a light.

It was blinding, impossible to look at directly no matter how hard Ax tried. It looked like a newborn star, beams of glowing orange and yellow sparking from it as she drew it from within her. It stayed in her hand for only a moment before rising to hover just above them. There was a stillness and silence as all held their breath. Then the tiny sun descended slowly, coming to rest just above the chest of the child in Nora's arms.

Haziel opened her eyes, the gleaming orb of light seeming to spark with renewed vigor as she stared at it. She opened her arms wide and embraced the energy as she had embraced Nora. Ax watched as the light pressed against her chest, then slowly sank within it.

There was a moment where time seemed to stop. The air ceased its spinning, the moon dimmed slightly in respect. Ax saw Ingard twitch out of the corner of his eye, ready to move to his sister's side at any second. Then Haziel began to glow.

Facets of color gleamed from her skin, in shades of orange, yellow and red. There was a sound like a great many bells, and Haziel was laughing. It was a joyous sound, pure and simple in its splendor. Nora was beaming down at the girl as she threw her head back in exalted giggles. The glowing began to dim, disappearing back within her all together as she opened her eyes to look into Nora's face. Bardro was hovering at her shoulder, face inquisitive.

"How do you feel?" he asked softly as Nora pushed a tendril of blonde hair from the child's face.

Haziel turned to him, eyes alight with a quality they had not contained mere moments ago. She raised a hand before him, palm up.

And a small star appeared from nothingness above it.

The noise slammed them from all sides: cheers, laughter, celebration. The Fae were beside themselves with excitement as Bardro gave Haziel the biggest smile Ax had ever seen. Ingard swept Haziel from Nora's arms, the two of them laughing as he spun her round and round. Velisa was weeping, tears falling across her own smile as she applauded with the rest.

In unison, the Zenoths raised their hands to their chests just as Nora had done. Ax concentrated on his core, just as Bardro had shown them previously. At once, he felt a fire within him. He could feel his magick splitting, parting with itself of its own accord as he drew two slivers of it from himself. His core vibrated intensely as he pulled his hand away, dragging the new cores out of his chest as he went.

It was a thing of beauty unknown before. Ax and his siblings stood surrounded by the Fae which they had created, two orbs of light held by each. The colors were all different, each magnificent in their own rights. The cores that Ax held were a vibrant shade of blue, crackling like lightning before a massive storm. The orbs of light rose from their outstretched hands, hovering overhead as the Fae continued to cheer. Then each core began to fly through the crowd, coming to rest with the beings whose souls called to them.

Ax watched his first core descend before Bardro's apprentice, Kivion. The blue glow lit his eyes and reflected off his wide grin as he embraced it. The Fae were beginning to glow as they accepted their magicks, just as Haziel had done. There were sparks of new magick making birth around them as the Fae began to work out their new gifts, but Ax was too focused on his second core to truly notice.

It was hovering in the air above Velisa and Ingard, both looking up to it with child-like wonder. Nora's second core had come to hover beside Ax's, neither moving as they became the last two without a host. Something was happening as they drew closer to one another. Ax could see Nora and Bardro fixated on the two as well, captivated by what was taking place.

The cores were drawing in to one another, spinning faster and faster as they seemed to fuse. The new magick was sending out tiny explosions of light, sparks of white, blue and gold cascading from it as the sound of bells began anew.

"By the Beyonds... Ax heard Bardro breathe as this mysterious new magick split itself once more into two individual cores. The cores came to rest before Velisa and Ingard, waiting.

There was a stunned silence, the Fae ceasing their magicks momentarily as all watched. Velisa's eyes flew to Ax's, hesitant as they were on the day of her birth into this world. He gave her a reassuring smile, certain that whatever this new thing was, it was surely a thing of greatness.

She beamed back at him, turning her eyes to Ingard as he took her hand in his. They embraced their cores in unison, the power disappearing within their chests in an instant. At once, they began to glow. Velisa was blue, bolts of lightning shooting from her fingertips and licking at the whites of her eyes. Ingard was a brilliant shade of white-gold, of what seemed to be beams of starlight circling up his impressive forearms.

Ax turned his gaze to Nora, whose eyes were already fixated on him. The look of soft reverence, of overwhelming love, told him that she felt just as he did: This was meant to be. And as the celebration kicked up fresh, the new magick users learning what their cores could do, the future of Zenafrost gleamed ever brighter.

And so it was that the Zenoths bestowed their blessing upon the Fae. The land has become more beautiful than ever before, aided by the magick that now fills most of the world. Those who chose to forgo the gift in hopes of a simpler life have risen great cities and townships across the continent, tending to farmland and raising livestock, settling down and creating offspring of their own.

The Fae that possess the gift have taken the Zenoth's magicks to new heights, harnessing powers the likes of which the cosmos have never seen. Those whose magicks share a common core are drawn together, both in friendship and in love, by forces beyond all comprehension. A soul tie seems to bind them, making these pairs the mightiest of all magick users.

So much is still left to discover, with new mysteries seeming to surface with every passing day. Bardro spearheads the hunt for answers to the many secrets Zenafrost holds. Mezilmoth, who had become fixated on the energy emanating from the core of the world, has yet to return from his crusade for knowledge.

As the Zenoths study Zenafrost, the world continues to evolve. Sentient life, unlike that which sprung from the Zenoth's combined magicks, rises from the lush landscape with untold awareness. And with this, a hidden shadow has made birth, threatening the lives of all who call Zenafrost home.

CHAPTER 3

THE BEGINNING OF THE END

It was barely dawn and Ax was already seated at his oaken desk, studying his copied version of Bardro's field journal with unmatched intensity. He had come to a segment on the orb lights that flitted across the whole of Zenafrost, pleased that Bardro had come to the same conclusions he himself had.

"Tufts of excess magick, watching us," Ax murmured to himself, eyes passing over the sentence explaining just this. "Studying us as we study them...but for what purpose, I wonder?"

The door behind him burst open, the journal dropping onto the desk as he startled. Velisa and Ingard rushed into the room, giggling and holding hands like children at play. This was how one would typically find them, ever since the blessing of the Zenoths. They were a tied pair, bonded as mates for life much like a pack animal might be. And there's was a special case, the magick cores within them merging unexplainably before they fused with their souls.

Ax sighed, holding his chest and grimacing, "One of these days, you'll stop my ancient heart from shock."

Velisa rolled her eyes, smirking as they approached the desk, "That would be quite the feat, considering you're a being of immortal cosmic energy." She perched on her usual poof by Ax's feet. "You'd have heard us coming, were you not so transfixed on rereading those field notes for the millionth time. Now, give us a smile Ax! We've got something new to show you."

Ax made a mocking face at her, but sat up straighter, eyes alight. Every time Velisa said this, it was followed by some fantastic new feat she and Ingard had discovered about their magicks. Unlike the stationary, unwavering magick of the Zenoths, the cores within the Fae tended to change with time and practice. Ever evolving, they were a point of great fascination for Ax. "Oh? Something more impressive than the veins of light you were able to create within the earth?"

Velisa beamed, "*Much* more impressive!" She stood from the poof, taking Ingard's outstretched hand and crossing the room to the open window. A narrow beam of sunlight was coming through, radiating from the first rays of morning. Velisa raised her free hand, placing it under the light. At once, the bright beam began to gather in a glowing pool in her palm.

It was something Ax had seen before, often followed by her using the gathered beams to spring flourishing plant life from the ground around her. Ax suspected this was due to some combined reaction from her powers mixing with the natural flow of magick throughout Zenafrost. Velisa threw him a wink, Ingard smiling at him as he too raised his free hand.

Ingard placed his palm against the side of the beam, angling it against Velisa's as one might lean against a wall. Ax watched as Ingard's eyes began to glow white. Then the beam of light fractured, radiating with the same ferocity as Ingard's stare. It burst from his hand, firing like a shooting star into the wall opposite.

Ax could hear the combined magick chiming like bells as he leapt from his seat, mouth open and eyes wide. "*Magnificent!*" he cried, clapping his hands as the beam began to spark tiny stars into the air around them. "*Incredible*! You've managed not only to harness the sun's light, but to actually *bend* it to your whim! Absolutely *incredible!*"

The beam had begun to shift in color, morphing through white to yellow to orange to red and back. There was a sound like cracking thunder, and tendrils of electricity whipped from the beam in a mad dance. Ax was beside himself with glee at the obvious power, even as the wall the beam struck began to smoke. A small fire burst to life on the wood as Velisa and Ingard struggled to withdraw their magick. By the time the beam dissipated, the fire had begun to spread across the wood lined wall.

"Sorry!" Ingard called, rushing forward. "*So* sorry!! We're still working on the dismount!" He let out a small laugh as he hurried towards the fire, waving one of his large hands out before it. The flames rose from the wood like smoke, vanishing into his palm as he absorbed them. Ax watched awestruck by this ability.

"That was an immense amount of power!" Ax was saying, studying the veins on Ingard's arm that still glowed like sunbeams. "To combine both your cores in such a way...truly spectacular! And you fully absorbing the fire?! When in the great Beyonds did you learn to do that?!"

Ingard shrugged, looking bashful as Velisa looked on with pride. "Well, I can't rightfully take credit for that. You remember how hard it was for me to control this thing at the beginning." He motioned to his chest, referencing the magick inside of him. "The electrical storms I caused, the fire I set in my home village while sun soaking five harvests past...It was difficult, and a little terrifying, if I'm being honest." He turned to Velisa with so much love in his eyes that Ax felt his own heart soar in the presence of it. "But Vel never gave up on helping me, never faltered no matter how many times I failed. I owe everything I am now to her."

Velisa blushed, waving her hand in embarrassment. "All I did was give you the right tools. The work you did with them was entirely your own, my love."

Ax patted Ingard's shoulder reassuringly, giving him a wink.

"Velisa is a special case. She's the only Fae we've seen so far that's exhibited near-flawless control of their gift."

"A wise man once said, 'We cannot achieve perfection, but there's no use trying if you're not striving to be damn near close.' Or something of the sort," Velisa said, smirking as Ingard returned to her side.

Ax chuckled, remembering this as his own words to Velisa on an expedition so many moons ago. "Whoever said that sounds incredibly wise. Probably quite handsome as well."

Velisa let out a hearty laugh. "Oh, you think so? I always thought he sounded like a giant ass---"

Ax made a face of mock outrage, picking up a crumpled piece of parchment from his desk and chucking it at her. The room was filled with laughter as Ingard used Velisa like a shield from Ax's paper onslaught. The door to the tower opened once more, and sudden warmth filled the room. Ax didn't need to turn around to know Nora had arrived.

"Sister!" he called, beaming as he approached her with open arms. She wore robes of yellow, the fabric trailing behind her like the rays of sunshine that spilled in around them. Her dark brown skin was adorned with all manner of jewelry and trinkets, most made by the hands of Fae children that had gifted them to her. She wore them with pride, always, each one special to her and worthy of their place upon her body. Bracelets trailed up to her elbow, anklets jangling together above her bare feet. Gems and rocks stretched her ears, pinned through the flesh like badges of her love. Atop her head sat a fresh crown of flowers, clearly given to her just the night before.

Nora embraced Ax, eyes filled with humor as she looked over his shoulder at Ingard and Velisa. "Without fail, if I cannot find one of you, I know I will always find the *three* of you together. Though, I did not expect *you* to be this awake so early, brother."

"You know Ax," Velisa replied, stepping forward to embrace Nora as well. "Can't keep him out of Bardro's journal for longer than it takes him to eat, most days."

Ax stuck his tongue out at her, stepping aside to allow Ingard the chance to bow before Nora. “I will not be shamed for my studies, Velisa. I find it imperative that I am on the same page as Bardro, in regards to our research. Speaking of which,” Ax raised an eyebrow at Nora, who was gazing at Ingard and Velisa like a mother would her children. “Have we received word from Mezilmoth? He must have filled a hundred journals by now with what he’s found. And Bardro suspects he’s delved into the caverns to the west at one point or another. He'd be the first to do so, and I’m hungry for whatever discoveries he’s surely made.”

Nora shook her head, looking sad at this. “Not a word from him since before the Ceremony of the Gift. Bardro has been able to pick up his trail now and again, which is the only reason we know he hasn’t ventured into the cosmos.”

Velisa cocked her head to the side, looking thoughtful. “I suspect he’s trying to glean all he can before returning to us. If he’s made it down into the earth, then perhaps he’s discovered something much larger than we have?”

Ax nodded. “I wouldn’t be surprised. He always was one step ahead of me and Bardro. I’d expect no less in his studies here.”

“Ah, that brings me to the matter at hand,” Nora said, returning her full attention to Ax. “Bardro has called upon us. He sent word to me on the winds before the sun rose this morning. He has discovered something vital and says that we must join him in the eastern forest at once.”

“What?!” Velisa and Ax said in unison, their excitement clear. Many of their biggest breakthroughs had come from Bardro’s ‘vital discoveries.’ Ax used his brother’s field journals as a priest might use a religious tome. Hours he spent with his nose pressed to the pages, making his own notes in the margins as he connected pieces of his own travels with Bardro’s. He had travelled much further than Ax, sat in observation far longer than either he or Velisa ever would with their diminished patience.

"A vital discovery?" Velisa repeated, bouncing on the balls of her feet with eyes alight.

"Like his encounters with the furies?" Ax added, referencing the last of Bardro's field research.

Nora chuckled, looking between the two of them. "The two of you are less kin, more clone. It's a wonder you've not begun to look alike."

Ax chuckled, throwing a mischievous side eye at Velisa. "Oh, she'd only be blessed with my stunning features in her wildest of dreams."

"You know, I was just about to say the same of *you*," she replied with a wicked grin.

"I suppose this means we'll be skipping breakfast then?" Ingard interjected, holding his stomach and looking slightly dejected.

Nora placed a loving hand on his shoulder, smiling. "The trees of the eastern forest bear tender and delicious fruits. They're sure to be ripe in this weather, my darling."

"And on our way, we can practice stemming the flow of our newest joined magick!" Velisa chimed in, wrapping her arm through Ingard's as they set off toward the tower door. "Wait until you see it, Nora! It nearly set the whole place ablaze this morning!"

THE EASTERN FORESTS were a place of great joy for Ax. It was here the Zenoths had first touched the grounds of this world they had created. Here that Velisa had emerged from the wood, the first Fae they encountered, crafted from the combined magick of the Zenoths and the cosmic dust that flowed through the whole of the universe. This place meant so much to him that this was where he chose to build the Library of Time. It stood just two hours walk from the borders of the vast eastern wood.

As the four approached, Ax was struck once more by its beauty. Multi-colored orb lights danced between vivid trunks of the same hues, each color melting into the last. It was always this way in spring when the wind was mellow and the sun kind on the skin. The trees would burst forth in these dazzling colors, flowers and fruits decorating their branches as far as the eye could see. The glow of the orb lights gave it an ever-mystical mystique that was only amplified by the magickal energy that poured from within the forest itself.

There, pacing the outer edge of the wood as they marched forward, was Bardro. He stopped pacing as they neared him with calls of enthusiastic greeting. Ax was the first to reach him, embracing his brother. "I've not seen you in ages, you great sod! You said you'd have your next journal to me *months* ago! You smell like stale salt water. When's the last you bathed?" Ax could feel the stiffness in Bardro's hug and pulled away. His brother's eyes were clouded, a look of grim severity on his face.

"Bardro...?" Nora said in a soft, hesitant voice from behind them.

"Tell us what's happened," Ax said in a low voice, all playful humor forgotten.

Bardro's face looked thinner than last they'd seen him. Great, dark circles were etched under his eyes, marking his lack of sleep. "You've told no one of our meeting?" he asked, gaze darting between the four of them.

Ax furrowed his brow in confusion and concern. "We came straight here, Bardro. What has happened?" he repeated.

Nora stepped forward, placing a hand on Bardro's shoulder with worried eyes. "Brother, tell us so we may face it---" She stopped short. Her eyes moved slowly from Bardro's face, widening. She stepped around him, expression vacant as she reached her hand towards the tree line.

There was a ripple of energy that reverberated through the warm air, winding Ax as Nora's fingers approached the border of the wood. Inches from passing into the forest's shadow, her hand suddenly stopped. She pressed her palm against what seemed to be an invisible wall, barring her from drawing any closer. "What..." she breathed, her hand still pressed firmly against the barrier.

Ax could feel it now. Overshadowed by the immense amounts of magick that came from the forest itself, he could sense heavy warding woven like a web across the forest. It stretched the length of the woods, extending far beyond where Ax could render. Mouth agape in disbelief, he dropped his gaze to his brother.

Bardro was standing with head bowed, the picture of shame. "We will be allowed to enter the wood, but only after I explain."

"*Allowed?*" Ax repeated, bewildered. He watched as Velisa and Ingard came to stand beside Nora, who looked hurt. Ingard took her free hand gently in his own, Velisa mirroring Nora as she placed her palm against the barrier.

Bardro looked up at him with the same darkened, haunted expression. "Please, brother. We have little time."

Ax bit his tongue. Never, in all their eternity together, had he ever seen Bardro act this way. The storm in his eyes wavered from wrath, to shame, to something that looked almost like fear. He gave a curt nod, folding his arms across his chest to keep himself silent.

Bardro glanced at Nora, who had returned her attention to him with a distant look. When he spoke next, it was with a softer tone. "The last we spoke, I was setting off to the shores just below this forest. I was intent on discovering what it was that hoarded such power beneath the waves. I sat for months upon that sand, examining and observing. Trying every which way to get even a small clue to lead me to an answer. And when I had all but given up, an answer finally came."

The wind rushed around them, swirling about Bardro as it whispered softly to him. Ax's eyes narrowed on the semi-visible gusts. His brother's unique control and relationship with the winds of Zenafrost was yet another thing of great mystery to him, and one Bardro had scarce answers to. The wind swept into the forest, vanishing as Bardro continued.

"A woman, a goddess created from the world itself, rose from the water. She appeared before me as a messenger for Zenafrost, to act as her voice."

His words were met with silence, the air unnaturally still.

"Zenafrost...the world is trying to speak to us?" Velisa asked quietly, looking thunderstruck.

"It *is* sentient," Ax breathed, eyes wide at this confirmation to his own theory.

Bardro nodded, solemn. "The creatures that are birthed from the earth call her 'The All Mother.' They're bound together by the magick that gives this world life. The ruler of the ocean, Brisën she is called...she came to me with grave warning. A darkness has been born unto Zenafrost. One that has set the lives of us all onto a path of destruction."

Ax felt his heart fall into the pit of his stomach. He stared at Bardro in disbelief, the look mirrored in Ingard and Velisa's pale faces.

Nora, in contrast, had straightened to her full and considerable height. All worry was gone from her eyes, replaced by an expression of deathly calm. Ax was reminded of a mother dragon protecting her kin as his sister's eyes flashed gold. "This darkness...is it within these woods?"

Bardro shook his head, "Brisën sent me here to find the ones she called 'earth born.' This barrier was raised to keep the darkness *out*." The wind whipped around him once more, whispering in many voices that were too faint for Ax to hear. Bardro nodded, and the winds shot back into the woods. "I think it's best if you hear it direct from the source. Or as close to it as possible." He motioned back towards the forest, towards where shadowy figures had begun to approach through the trees.

Ingard stepped beside Velisa, squaring his shoulders in defense. Ax felt the tension in the air, his jaw clenched in anticipation.

Three beings stepped through the forest's shield, coming to stand before them. Ax stared in awe. From a distance, one might mistake them as Fae. Their tall statures, characteristic points to their ears, and natural beauty were just the same. But here was where the similarities ended. These were not creatures born of the Zenoths, instead looking to have been risen from the very earth beneath their feet.

They each exuded a tremendous amount of raw magick, the same kind that emitted from the very heart of Zenafrost. The first had skin the color of pale roses, tendrils of silken vines flowing like hair from their head. Their fingers were wrapped in flower petals, each jointed to bend with the movement of their body. Their eyes glowed a vibrant shade of green that reminded Ax of freshly sprung grass.

The second could have been a stone statue, had their chest not been moving with breath. Their gray and white body looked carved straight from rock brought to life. Crystal formations, pulsing with every imaginable color, formed a crown atop their head, and their eyes were white as fallen snow.

The last seemed to have been made of the trees that filled the vast wood. Though their skin was made of bark, it looked somehow as soft as velvet. Their arms led down to branch-like fingers, each tipped in newly born leaves. A large bush of flowers served as their hair, drifting discarded petals lazily across their violently red eyes. Though all three were void of clothing, they lacked any visible signs of gender.

The one made of roses bowed their head gracefully. "Children of the Cosmos, we bid thee welcome."

Their voice was strange, resonating in three distinctly different tones as they spoke. The beings of rock and wood bowed as well, dropping their heads low in respect.

"What are you?" Ax said, eyes still wide in shock as he took in their appearances. These were not like the animals and strange, watchful orb lights that had sprung from Zenafrost in the past. This was something Ax had never seen before, never thought *possible.*

The one made of stone smiled at him, the crystals upon their head winking with light. "We are those born from the Green Womb, risen from the soil of All Mother as products of her growing magick. You may call us Forest Dwellers." Their voice too sounded as three, mimicking the first. Though the predominant tone of this one was much lower.

"The Green Womb is a grove near the heart of their forest," Bardro explained quickly, watching the confusion pass across their shocked faces. "I suspect it lies just over the heart of Zenafrost. The magick there is the most concentrated I've ever felt."

The Forest Dweller who looked made of trees nodded in response to this. "Yes. The Womb is flush with great and cosmic power. We are the first to rise, but we are far from the last."

"Why have you barred us from the wood?" Velisa said, the hurt she felt clear in her voice. The forest was where she had taken her first breaths as well, and Ax could see anger roiling beneath her stare at being kept from it.

The Forest Dwellers drew their attention towards her in perfect unison, and Velisa drew back slightly from the intensity in their shared gaze. All three opened their mouths and began to speak as one. "A darkness has begun to rise, hidden and quick. It grows in silence, corrupting the life that is pure and light. The threads of destiny fray against it, fray as it poisons the All Mother and all that come from her. The fate of all that call her home has been threatened."

The air grew cold, the wind unmoving as they stood in shock. Then Ingard let out a small laugh. "That can't be. We've travelled far and wide and seen no such pall on the land."

"The darkness is hidden in the veins of the world, for now." Bardro replied, the hopeful look disappearing from Ingard's face. "The corruption works unseen, but rest assured: it will not stay so for long. I have felt it for myself, far in the mountains to the east. It absorbs all that is good. Strangles it. *Changes* it." He spoke the last words with such haunting remembrance that Ax couldn't help but shiver in response.

"Where does it come from?" Nora demanded, the fire still burning in her golden eyes. "What has brought it upon us?"

The rose-made Forest Dweller answered. "Though a thing of

great beauty and devotion, it was the gift the Zenoths gave unto the Fae that has set us on this course."

Nora looked like she had been slapped across the face. Ax shook his head, refusing to believe it. "No. Impossible. I have met and studied each of the Fae who partook of the gift. I would have noticed if something was amiss."

"No, brother," Bardro said, his voice low, "it is not a Fae that brings this threat upon us. It is a Zenoth."

It was like a dagger to the heart. Nora let out a gasp, Ax feeling winded once more as his mind reeled. "One of *us?*"

The mixture of wrath and shame that had been threatening to take over Bardro's face spilled forth at once. "When we arrived here, we all noted how powerful the natural flow of magick was. And when we introduced our magicks to this already-potent atmosphere, it created something new entirely. Something mightier than any of us had ever seen. And though most of us took this as a blessing, and as something beautiful and new to learn from, one of us did not."

The oaken Forest Dweller continued as Bardro's fury caused his words to fail. "The All Mother is ever watchful. She felt when the first ripples of corruption shook the magick of our world. Selfish greed and prideful arrogance have tainted that which was once pure. Magick has begun to change across all of Zenafrost."

"It was this that prompted us to raise this barrier," the stone Forest Dweller continued, motioning behind them towards the woods. "We must ward the forest and keep the heart of the All Mother protected. At all costs."

"This darkness," Ingard said, his voice uncharacteristically cold, "will it affect everyone in Zenafrost? Magick and non-magick users alike?"

The Forest Dwellers nodded in unison, looking sad.

"Can you not extend your wards?!" Velisa said, the panic in her eyes growing, "Protect everything that's still untouched by the darkness?"

"I've already asked all these questions," Bardro said in a muted tone. "Their magick can only do so much. It's taking all they have to hold these barriers in place."

"We have to do something," Ingard growled, his expression darker than Ax had ever seen it. "My family lives in a village close to the western mountains. Their right in the path of whatever this darkness is."

"We'll go straight there," Velisa reassured him, and Ax watched as she overrode her own frantic fear to settle the anxiety gripping Ingard. "If we can't bring the barrier to them, then we'll bring everyone to the barrier." Her eyes shifted to the Forest Dwellers, her gaze unfaltering. "I trust you will allow us to do so."

The Forest Dwellers bowed in unison, before speaking as one. "We would have it no other way, Child of the Sun."

"Hiding will not stop the darkness from consuming all it can," Ax said, feeling a fire rising within him. "This is our *home*. We created this world, brought our magicks to bear upon her soil. And if one of us has fallen, it is our duty to set it right."

"Time runs short," the rose Forest Dweller said, gazing up at the clear afternoon sky that stood in such stark difference to their perilous conversation. "What happens next is unknown to us, but the destiny of Zenafrost is entangled with the fates of *all* across the cosmos. Should we lose to it here, the universe too shall fall."

Bardro stood tall, his aura exuding command. "One of our own threatens to undo all we have created. All we hold dear to us." His eyes flickered momentarily to Velisa and Ingard, the fear once again sparking deep within them. This was not fear of the darkness, Ax realized, but fear of what might happen to the Fae. It was an emotion that shot through him like ice in his veins as Bardro continued. "We must root out the corruption, cleanse them of its grasp. We must call our kin to the Chamber of the Sun."

With the warning of Zenafrost laying heavy on their hearts, those present in the woods that day set out on their quests. Their mission was simple: find the source of the darkness and end it.

Before it ended them.

Velisa and Ingard took off towards the villages to silently ready the Fae for whatever may come. Nora, Ax, and Bardro found themselves faced with a grave task. A Zenoth, one of their own kin, had brought corruption to the purity of magick. Unable to trust any but themselves, each split off to a separate corner of the world, desperately searching for any sign of threat. Weeks, months, years passed, with nothing to show but growing tensions and fear.

Though Velisa and Ingard chose to keep the dire threat from their people, the Fae were not easily fooled. They could sense something on the horizons. Even those without a magick core could feel the change in the wind.

And on one fateful Autumn's Eve, Bardro sent word to Nora and Ax. A letter that simply read:

Call our kin to the Chamber of the Sun. I have found the darkness.

CHAPTER 4
THE FALL

The light of the Chamber was surreal against Ax's tired eyes. How long had it been since they had gathered here? Five? Six hundred years? Cold sweat beaded his brow and his pulse echoed in his head. He felt sure all those present around him would hear it. That it would signal whoever the culprit was to their suspicions.

Ax gulped, forcing his breath to steady. He had spent the last several years tirelessly chasing shadows and rumors from one end of Zenafrost to the next. He couldn't recall the last time he had slept, the last time he had studied in the field for pure enjoyment's sake. The last time he saw Velisa, she was thin and drawn, a reflection of Ax's own stark visage. Ingard and her efforts to train the Fae for battle had weighed heavy on their shoulders. A weight that had only been made heavier with their inability to find the source of the coming darkness.

Across the Chamber from him, surrounded by blissfully chattering Zenoths, was Nora. Her face was lit up as she spoke to one of their brothers, though Ax knew it was only a ruse. Nora had been more bent on finding the darkness than perhaps anyone. Ax had scarcely seen her since their encounter with the Forest Dwellers, and she had been clear of her intent when they had last spoke. She sought to find their corrupted kin and save them from themselves, 'heal them' from their darkness, as she had called it.

Bardro had told her vehemently that this was likely impossible.

"If this darkness is as mighty as the Dwellers warn," he had said to her gently, "then our only hope would be to bind our corrupted kin to the Great Crystal."

Ax's eyes fell on the crystal at the center of them all. The Zenoths had been born from the crystal, stepped forth from within its vast cosmic energy. The Great Crystal was the only thing in the known universe that could end their immortal life for good.

The thought of using it, of ending the life of one of his kin...it was too much to even consider. It made him sick, forcing his eyes shut to stem the waves of dizzying nausea.

"I just can't work it out."

Ax jumped, disrupting a cloud of stardust that exploded in a thousand tiny faucets around him. He covered his mouth to contain the yelp, whipping around to the direction of the voice.

His sister, Friya, sat beside him. She had appeared out of nothingness, or perhaps Ax had been too consumed in his dark musings to hear her arrival. She raised an eyebrow, looking grim. "You do know my power is prophecies, correct?"

Ax blinked at her, clearing his throat and evening his expression. "How could I forget? You've predicted every solar event, every massive energy flux, every flicker of destiny to ever be." Ax knew all of this, but his heart fell as he said it aloud. *Her power is prophecies,* he thought. *She tells the future, and we've tried to keep this hidden from her all-seeing eye.*

Friya scowled at him. "And yet the three of you didn't think to come to me for help?" She threw a reproachful look over at Nora. "Here I thought I was alone in my torment."

"Your torment?" Ax lowered his voice, leaning towards her. "Do you mean to tell me you've...you've *seen* it? The threat to

Zenafrost...?" He chose his words carefully, still uncertain on who was to blame.

Friya's brow furrowed. This close, Ax could see the nearly black circles under her eyes. "My first vision happened a year ago. I thought it was a nightmare when it happened. I saw Zenafrost, but it was not as it is now. The land was baren and cracked, destroyed by a darkness that I couldn't...I couldn't comprehend..." She trailed off for a moment, looking worn and frightened. "I've since had many visions of what is to come, but none are clear. A great shadow covers what I truly seek."

"The identity of the corruptor," Ax whispered this, his voice strangled.

Friya nodded slowly in return. "It feels purposeful. Like whatever it is holds enough power to hide themselves, even in a future that has yet to pass." She drew her wide eyes to meet Ax's. "Brother, I know not what to do. I see all...I have never *not* known what is to come. I feel as if...as if something *terrible* is about to happen." She shuddered at this, her body trembling.

Ax placed his hand over hers, squeezing it gently. "That is why we have come to the Chamber, Friya. Bardro has found the source of the corruption. After today, it will be a thing of cruel memory and yes, of nightmares." The portal across from them lit up, drawing Ax's attention away from his trembling sister.

Mezilmoth stepped through, and an invisible weight lifted from Ax's shoulders. Though his eldest brother had been away on his own expeditions, out of reach of their attempted contacts, Ax felt sure he would be of invaluable use in what was to come. He looked more alive than ever, his silver hair flowing freely to his waist and his eyes alight with their hungry curiosity. Ax wondered what new knowledge he held, what stories he could tell him when this was all over. Mezilmoth smiled as he caught Ax's stare, winking before turning to stride towards Nora.

Nora beamed at her brother and Ax got the impression that she felt the same relief that he had upon seeing Mezilmoth. The Zenoths surrounding stepped aside in respect as their brother swept past. Nora held her arms wide in welcome, her sunshine-like glow pulsing from her skin for the first time in months.

Crack.

A flash of light blinded the Zenoths as a sound like cracking earth filled the Chamber. The light vanished and gasps rang out. Bardro had appeared from thin air, positioned in a defensive stance between Nora and Mezilmoth. Ax felt a ripple of energy and recognized it as a shield rising around Nora.

"You will move no closer," Bardro's voice was feral, more beast than cosmic-being.

The energy in the chamber shifted. The air grew unnaturally still, the crystal, which was ever turning, slowed by just a fraction. Ax felt ice cold, unable to pull his eyes away from the scene unfolding before them.

Bardro let out a noise that sounded like a wild animal, ripping from his throat as he continued to hold his ground before Nora.

Mezilmoth stared at him blankly, hand still half extended in offer to his eldest sister. For a long moment, Ax was able to convince himself that it was a dream, or perhaps a cruel trick. But then Mezilmoth smiled.

It was not the smile he remembered on his brother's perfect face. This was a thing of merciless hatred, veiled in unhinged triumph. He let out a laugh that was as cold as the Chamber was becoming. Something was terribly wrong. *Run, run, run.* A voice within Ax was begging him to flee, begging him to run to the furthest corner of the universe and never look back. The Great Crystal had stopped spinning all together, hovering as if in wait for whatever was coming next. The air was heavy, the usual blinding brightness of the Chamber replaced by an eerie grey hue.

Mezilmoth cocked his head at Bardro, his eyes void of all light. "I should have known you'd be the first to find me out. To be frank, I thought you would have sorted it out much sooner. I've been keeping my true form hidden for years; it's been most tiring."

And a sudden wall of dark energy slammed into the Zenoths.

It emanated from Mezilmoth, filling the Chamber in an instant. The hovering walls of white stone began to crack, the very atmosphere trembling against the darkness. Bardro shot a bolt of bright, white magick towards Mezilmoth. He waved a hand lazily, and the bolt collided with a shield of pure shadow before him. It disappeared in an instant, amidst the collective gasp from the Zenoths. Ax's eyes were wide, disbelieving even as he watched.

Mezilmoth raised an eyebrow, looking at Nora standing dumbstruck behind Bardro. "Oh, don't look so surprised, dear sister. Surely you must have felt it. I *know* you have, or else you wouldn't have come looking. The shift in energy, the growing of my powers...evolution at play, in the finest way."

"This is not evolution. It is *madness*," Bardro snarled at him, silently beginning to raise protective shields around his siblings as he held Mezilmoth's gaze.

Mezilmoth let out another cold, cruel laugh. "Madness? You dare speak to me of madness when you turn a blind eye to the power we have created? The power that is rightfully *ours* for the taking?" He spun slowly in place, addressing the Chamber at large now. "Soullings! We stand at the precipice of destiny! It is by divine direction we were brought here to this place, to this home that holds magick beyond even our understanding! Think of the possibilities, the potential for true greatness! This is what we are meant for!"

"We were meant to bring love and light to the cosmos." The words spilled from Ax before he could stop them. "What you speak of is everything we would stand against."

Mezilmoth clicked his tongue disapprovingly at Ax. "I was worried you'd all see it this way. You just haven't developed enough to understand the way I do. And that's alright, brother. I will show you. I will show you *all* what true power is."

Tendrils of smoke began to billow forth from Mezilmoth's flesh, surrounding the Chamber in the space of a heartbeat. Instantly, the walls began to crumble. The light vanished, replaced by black darker than the most starless night. Even the constellations above them disappeared, consumed by the void.

There was a mighty ringing sound, and light was erupting from Nora and Bardro. They held hands, covering their siblings in a protective dome of sunbeams and stardust. The darkness pulsed against the barrier, probing, searching for a way in.

Mezilmoth looked amused. "I will offer you this only once. Kneel before me, as the rightful ruler of the cosmos. Sit at my side as I bring the universe together as one. Join me in this next leap and we will ascend to our greater purpose *together*."

"We will not kneel, brother," Nora's voice echoed through their heads, overtaking every thought. "Our purpose is to bring others to stand beside us. Not to reign above them. Your heart has lost its way."

Mezilmoth had turned to face her, a hatred in his eyes that Ax had never seen before. *He's going to kill her,* the voice within him cried. *He has fallen to his madness, and he is going to kill her.* And, as Mezilmoth set his mirth on Nora, Ax took his moment.

Before Mezilmoth had the chance to turn, Ax had leapt from behind the barrier. With a strangled cry of sorrow, he shot a stunning beam of vibrant blue electricity straight at his brother.

It struck him in the chest, right at his heart. Mezilmoth gasped, stumbling slightly in the air as the darkness wavered. He looked at Ax with stunned betrayal. "You? Of all others, *you* were the one I saw as my right hand. The one I saw forever at my side." Then all emotion vanished from his eyes. It was replaced by swirling, impossible darkness.

"Get back, Ax!" Bardro cried, blasting a ball of light towards Ax that threw him back behind the barrier. And not a moment too soon. The darkness increased tenfold, deafening in its pressure.

"He mustn't touch the crystal!" Friya cried out from somewhere through the void.

At once, Ax raised his hands in attack. The second time in his entire existence that he had to do so. He felt his siblings gathering their magick about them as well, a combined force that was fired in soundless tandem. They aimed at the place Mezilmoth had been, their beams striking the darkness away on impact. In the clearing brought by their magick, they could see the Chamber of the Sun again.

It had been decimated; all previous splendor reduced to blackened ruin around them. Mezilmoth was standing before the Great Crystal, still frozen in place between them all. The Zenoths joint attack had been stopped short, cracking around an invisible barrier that surrounded their brother.

His face looked oddly stretched, elongated, and distorted as he smiled wickedly at them all. His eyes were completely black, staring directly at Ax as he reached out a hand.

"No!" Bardro and Nora cried out in unison as Mezilmoth laid his palm atop the crystal. There was a spine-tingling zap of energy that set Ax's teeth on edge.

And then the crystal exploded.

The force blasted into the Zenoths, sending them all flying in scattered directions. Ax saw Bardro fighting against the impossible waves of power, flying with rage filled eyes back to the place where Mezilmoth had stood. But he vanished into the ether beyond, leaving nothing but chaos and cold laughter in his absence.

The Zenoths gathered around each other slowly, as if in a daze. Ax could scarcely believe it had happened. The Chamber was gone. The crystal that birthed the Zenoths, grew their magick, shattered. Some of Ax's siblings were crying, all looking as lost as he felt. But Bardro was looking positively murderous. Even so, he softened his steel gaze and turned to Nora.

She was standing still as stone, tears streaming down her face as she took in the nothingness. "How could we let this happen?"

Bardro's lip curled in anger, eyes flashing. "We were betrayed." He turned to face the Zenoths, placing a hand on Nora's shoulder to steady her. "We've *all* been betrayed. Mezilmoth has fallen into darkness. Without the Great Crystal to bind him..." He trailed off, and Ax watched a flicker of fear pass below the wrath in his gaze. "He has yet to unearth the workings of Zenafrost. He cannot use her magicks, and therein lies our only advantage. We must protect our home. Our people."

Friya whimpered beside Ax. All the color had drained from her face. When she spoke, it was with a voice barely above a whisper. "This is it. This is what I saw in my vision. The beginning of the end."

Ax's hands clenched into fists so tight, his fingernails dug deep into his palms. "This is not the end. It *cannot* be. Bardro is right. Mezilmoth has yet to figure out how to harness the magick of Zenafrost. We must find him and stop him before he can." He turned from his unraveling siblings, one thought pushing all others from his mind as he began to lead them at lightspeed through the cosmos: down towards Zenafrost.

I must protect Velisa. He cannot be allowed to harm our people.

Mezilmoth

CHAPTER 5
ALL I EVER WANTED

I remember it, being born. I was everything and nothing before I emerged from within the crystal's walls. I remember Nora, waiting for me and glowing like the sun with her unending acceptance of her truths. I remember ***purpose.*** Before sound and feeling and light, I could sense I was here for something. Something dire and gripping. "You are here to spread joy and happiness," Nora told me. "You are here to spread love."

Love.

The universe was vast, dark, and blinding all at once. I was overwhelmed by the things I saw. I was driven by the need to understand them, to understand ***it*** all. Why do the trees grow? Why does the wind whistle? What controls the waters that spring from the magick in my core?

And my magick...what was it? What was its purpose, ***my*** purpose? I found the answers to all my questions. My magick was wrought of crystal ether and stardust. It could give life to plant and flora, could breathe music into the breeze. It was I that controlled the tide, on every world I ever built or studied. Nothing was out of my reach on these planets, no secret or stone untouched. Undisturbed.

And it was not long before I was simply, unwaveringly, bored. I returned to the Chamber, to Nora with her glowing light and dream of something *more.* I tried to settle. I lent my skills and newfound wisdoms to my kin; taught Bardro and Axoliphim how to peel apart the very fabrics of the worlds they created to get to the very soul within. And for a time, I began to believe this was it. My grand, damned 'purpose.'

But then came Zenafrost.

From the moment my feet touched her warm earth, I knew she was different. This was not like the other worlds my kin had created. This was something...something *living.* I could sense veins of magick, pumping like blood to a heart that spoke to me. The core of Zenafrost welcomed us with open arms. The life we had created, the Fae that sprang from our magicks... they were secondary to this all-powerful entity. The gift was not these Fae, no. It was Zenafrost herself. And I felt the pull of "purpose" once more.

I set off at once. There was a pace I kept when unlocking the secrets of a place. I've peeled worlds apart bit by bit until they were laid bare and open before me. But Zenafrost demanded more respect than this. She wasn't unfeeling; she knew every stone I flipped, every cave I dove into in search of her core. At first she was willing, seeming to lead me down the paths that would take me to the answers I sought. But what she gave me was surface. A mere shadow of what I knew hid beneath the layers of stone and dirt and vine and root. I offered her my magick, my *knowledge* in return for more. Just a little more. But soon, the winds ceased to whisper their tales to me. The oceans thrashed when I tried to cross them, the creatures stopped coming to me of their own accord. I had to resort to traps, a crude and crass thing, to continue my intensive studies.

The more I dug, the more I could feel Zenafrost pulling away. As if her mysteries, the mysteries that *we* created and brought to life, were hers to covet. It didn't make sense. Why keep such wisdom and power in a hoard to herself? It was selfish. *She* was selfish. I could dig no further, for she would not allow me. Her magick formed some sort of shield around her core and hid it entirely from my eyes. I needed to understand the magick of this world better if I was ever to unlock those final doors she had forced so tightly shut.

It was by pure mistake and happy happenstance when my first guide came to me. He was a traveler, a Fae from one of the western villages. He had been setting off to build a new life on the eastern shores when he had run afoul of a wandering Mountain Fury. Even with his borrowed magick, given to him by one of my kin, he stood no chance against the beast's might. When I came across him, he was on the very precipice of death. Half-crushed, weeping, unable to beg me for the help he so clearly needed. And when I approached, it was with the intent of healing him. He would have survived and gone on to live a happy life with his brethren. But when I knelt beside this traveler, I saw it.

The magick core in his heart, so very similar to that of my own, was morphed. It was as if vines had tangled themselves about the magick, lacing it with remnants of the very life that pulsed within Zenafrost. This magick core had been touched by her somehow. I had never been this close to the veins of power I so desperately desired. And I was stunned. The closer the man came to death, the brighter the core pulsed. It looked like a trapped bird, begging to be free of its cage. I did what anyone would have done, faced with the thrashing mess.

I reached into the traveler and pulled the core from him with my bare hands.

I thought it might take flight somehow. Burst into the air and sky and vanish from me just like the soul of the dead traveler at my feet. But instead, the magick nestled into my palm. It melted into my flesh, and I could feel it become one with my own.

I had never felt such power. This was beyond purpose, surely. This...this was *destiny*. This was the "love" Nora always spoke of. I knew that with this new magick, I could do things the other Zenoths had never even dreamed of. Could not even comprehend, in their shallow depth of vision. I needed more. If I was to do the things I needed, to harness the fabrics of Zenafrost in all she was, I would need much, much more.

It was only a few Fae. Travelers, just like the first. Lost, wandering, searching. Searching, of course, until they found me. Their sacrifices were fated. Our paths crossed for a reason, and that reason was to bring them into this journey. The more power I collected and cores I obtained, the clearer my purpose became. What I was meant for extended beyond Zenafrost's mysteries. No, I needed the core of Zenafrost for a much grander purpose indeed.

In my studies before coming to this world, I had learned one thing that always eluded me: there were other cosmos beyond our own. Cosmos I could not touch with my meager magicks. They held life. Life that had yet to be discovered, yet to be learned about and understood. But with the core that hid within Zenafrost...with her heart, I could do anything. I could reach those lives too. Just as I had done here.

I began to notice a change in myself. The more magick I absorbed, the stronger this change became. Things I touched grew blackened: plant, animal, fae. Like my shadow became a part of them somehow. Like this change in my core magick changed the composition of lesser things. I wondered at the extent of this spreading shadow. At the extent of this change.

I couldn't dissect myself. I wasn't even sure where to start if I could. I had become so much more than I was before. There were so many layers to what I was now. To where I was going. There was only one thing for it. I took on an apprentice. A like-minded Fae, an outcast for his own unbridled and untamed magicks. His core ran wild within him, causing chaos and destruction. No one helped. No one cared. But I did. I found him, lost as the others, and looking for exactly what I was: *purpose.*

I brought him to the place I had been using as my study. A great cavern that I had blasted deep into Zenafrost, in a failed search for her hidden core. It was the perfect spot to launch my experiment. My apprentice, Normigone, was more than willing. The promise of great power, of *my* power, was all he needed to join me. Below the bogs in the west, shrouded by the dizzying mists, we descended. We stood in the center of the great chasm I had created, stood hand in hand as I infused this Fae with my newly made magick.

I overestimated what his mind, what his *soul* could handle and contain. Indeed, my magick affected his core. Its very essence changed and evolved into something akin to what I had created within myself. But Normigone was no Zenoth. As my magick swept through him, I could feel something inside of his mind snap. I can't place exactly what it was, but it was drastic enough to leave him nearly mad. He spoke of shadow beings moving inside of him. That he could feel them crawling beneath his skin, begging to be released. It reminded me of that first traveler. Of the thought of a bird being trapped in his core. Over those next few days, he became consumed with this notion, obsessed with the need to release the things that seemed to torment him so.

This was when my next realization struck. The other Zenoths, my bloodlings and kin...they would not understand this. This greater purpose I had assumed. They would take one look at Normigone and any others like him and claim I was lost. But what did they know of the lost? Bardro, with his surface-level studies. Axoliphim in his gilded tower of knowledge. And Nora, oh Nora. She would be the worst of them all. I could see her face, condescending and understanding all at once when she told me I would have to be locked away until I was "purified." I was intimate with the lost, with the forgotten, with the cast aside. They preached their "love" but turned a blind eye to these souls who were falling through the cracks of this world. It was I who gave those lost souls purpose. I who gave them a home. And this was my second realization: the lost outweighed the found. If my destiny was to reach these new cosmos, these new worlds, then should it not also be that my destiny is to save those not yet reached? To give them, as I had done the lost souls of Zenafrost, a greater purpose? Was this not what "love" was supposed to be? I loved the Fae, I loved Zenafrost, and I loved those of the worlds I had yet to see. I loved them so much that I wished nothing more than to give them this greatest gift: to lead them to a better, a brighter, tomorrow. It was not *I* who did not understand devotion. It was *them.* Their love was selfish, conditional as long as the Fae followed their teachings. I would love without weight; I would save them without expectations.

I could see the path unfolding before me. Yes, I could see it then, clearer than ever before. No matter which way I spun it, there was no avoiding their interruption of my plans. They would not see the obvious hands of destiny at work. They would see only through their own clouded veils of wispy judgment. They would take the only plausible action, in their eyes. The only thing that could contain my power now, the only thing that could stop my magick, was the very crystal that brought me into this life. Suspended in the Chamber of the Sun, they would strip me of all I was. Of everything I had become and fought so hard to be. And I could not stand for it. I *would not* stand for it.

I would give them the chance, of course. I would offer them their rightful places beside me in the journey to come. We are gods, after all. We were born for this, this very thing that I intend to do. And perhaps some would see my truth, would see past the fog that was Nora and her severe, blinding 'light.' The others would fall in line with them. Or I would uncreate them, just as I intended to do with the crystal in the Chamber. Without it, they had no hope of stopping me. No means of standing in the way of fate. And this was the fate of not only the Zenoths, but of *all* under the Great Beyonds.

I remember being born. I remember it well. The Mezilmoth of then, lost and confused, would be so proud of who I am now. For I finally understand. I understand everything.

In the wake of the Chamber of the Sun's decimation, Mezilmoth was first to return to Zenafrost. His corrupted magick kept his power safe from the loss of the Great Crystal, while his kin began at once to feel the grave consequences. The magick that had once granted them the ability to create entire worlds had already started to flicker, the first cries of the dying light. Mezilmoth had made his dark intentions clear, and though his powers kept him shielded from the Zenoths frantic search, the earth showed his corruption everywhere he tread. He was more powerful than all the magick the Zenoths had left, and his abilities only grew with each passing day. They knew they stood no chance of ending him now that the Crystal was gone. But Bardro had learned of a way to seal him, to trap him away in a place where he could never harm another world. Only together did they stand a chance against his coming war. Only together could they hope to save the cosmos.

CHAPTER 6
THE CALL TO ARMS

Ax hadn't realized just how many lives now called Zenafrost home. Though, he supposed, it had been many thousands of years since the first Fae walked the green soils. It only stood to reason that there were this many generations now. Hundreds of thousands stood in the great fields below the mountains. The buzz of voices echoed all around, the tone consistent and fearful. Magick and non-magick users alike could feel the shift in the air, could sense the darkness that loomed. Ax could see the faces of Forest Dwellers dotted amongst them, stoic in comparison to the anxious Fae. Ax's stomach dropped. How were they going to keep them all safe?

He looked around to his kin, standing shoulder to shoulder with their backs to the mountain. He could see a vast array of emotion: anger, sadness, betrayal, pain. These were all feelings that squeezed tight around his own heart, strangling him. The usual glow that exuded from the Zenoths had begun to fade, disappearing slowly with their magicks. Ax turned from his agonized siblings. His eyes came to settle on Ingard and Velisa, standing before the sea of Fae and Forest Dwellers. Ax knew they were afraid, but you could see no hint of it on their faces. They looked nothing short of mighty leaders, attempting to calm their people before the truth of their fears were realized. Ax swallowed hard, fighting back the sudden urge to weep.

"I beg of you to listen to me," Nora's voice echoed, magnified above all others. She stood beside Ax, chin tilted to the sky and shoulders set back in a pose of resolute decision. "I know you are afraid. We will keep you safe, but you all must listen."

The Fae and Forest Dwellers grew silent at once, and an unnatural hush swirled around them on the breeze. All eyes were fixed on Nora, who stood somehow taller under their bated breaths.

"Is it true?!" A frantic voice cried from somewhere in the crowd. "Have one of you turned against us?!"

There was an outcry of voices once more, angry and scared. Ax could hear children sobbing, could hear mothers and fathers trying to console them through the noise.

Nora bowed her head in shame. "Our brother, Mezilmoth, has fallen to a darkness we cannot fathom."

The volume of the crowd increased tenfold.

"And you allow him to walk amongst us? To endanger our families? Our lives?" said another Fae voice in the crowd, whose statements were met with cheers of agreeance.

"Mezilmoth took great care to gut our powers at the source," Nora explained, looking hurt. "We are not capable of ending him-"

The rest of her sentence was cut short by the wave of noise from the angry crowd. Ax did not blame them for their fury, nor their pointed wrath towards the Zenoths for their inability to stop this coming evil. He looked to Nora, whose face was still painted in shame.

"*Enough.*" It was Ingard's voice now raising louder than the immense crowd. He strode to the front of the line of Zenoths, Velisa following in step. They faced the sea of thousands with heads held high. "These are our friends. Our *family.* Are you so quick to lay blame on the whole of them for one corrupted fruit?" The deep bass of his tone practically shook the ground on which they stood. The crowd had fallen silent once more.

"They have brought us here to discuss their plan," Velisa added, her jaw clenching. "We all live on this world together. And this is a fight we must overcome in the same." She turned and nodded back at Nora, Ingard and herself stepping to the side.

"There is a way," Bardro spoke into the renewed silence from his place on the other side of Nora. "A way to stop Mezilmoth and seal him in a place beyond this world. Beyond all worlds." He paused, allowing this reassurance to wash over the crowd. "It is true: my brother has fallen to this darkness that grew within him. We...*I* should have seen it. Should have stopped it before it could take him..." He trailed off, sounding choked.

Ax took up the mantle, "*None* of us saw the corruption that felled him. But fall he did. We will not lie to you: what he seeks is domination over not only Zenafrost, but of all who live in the cosmos. It is an evil plan, and one that I fear will bring about great bloodshed on all fronts." A cold chill passed through them, raising goosebumps across Ax's skin. But he continued with steady voice. "I tell you this not to frighten you, but to ready you. War is coming. We can all feel it. Mezilmoth cannot be killed, but he can be *bound.* There is a realm between realms...a dimension at the end of all things. We seek to tear through the fabric of our reality, and seal Mezilmoth away in that place."

Whispers took up throughout the crowd as he said this.

"We will lead him to the very edge of Zenafrost," Bardro continued. "The rift will be placed there, where none can reach it. When Mezilmoth is safely inside, we will seal it shut and ward the gate. He will still have his powers, but he will have no way to reach the lives of those he seeks to rule."

"Then it is war he seeks?" A voice in the crowd called. It silenced the growing whispers.

"Yes," Nora replied softly. "And I am so sorry. So very sorry that it has come to this. But know we will do everything we can to keep you all safe. I would do so with my dying breath..." Her voice trembled and Ax took her hand, squeezing it tight.

A woman stepped forward from the sea of bodies. She was dressed in pale yellow, her short-cropped brown hair tied back with a scrap of cloth. She came to stand before the Zenoths, her face resolute.

"Zenafrost is my home," she said. "A threat to one is a threat to all. I will fight beside you, and anyone else who should stand with us. For our world."

A man strode forward to join her, head held high. "For our families. For our future, and the future of all."

They were the two that started the flood. The crowd surged forward, letting out battle cries and shouts of furious power. Ax could not fight the tears that welled in his eyes, tears of both great pride and great fear. He could see the future of his people on the darkening horizon behind them. Many would be lost in the battles to come, on all sides. That much, at least, was promised.

But in this moment, in this one glorious moment of togetherness as the hundreds of thousands joined in a huge embrace, Ax felt that maybe...maybe their plan wasn't so impossible after all. If anything could defeat the darkness, it would surely be this fierce and overwhelming love. He found himself grasping Velisa and Ingard tightly to himself, feeling their tears soaking through his tunic. He would do anything to save them. Anything to save them *all.*

Zenafrost is at war. The skies grow darker each day. At the epicenter of battle, the earth is stained red with blood. The destruction of the Chamber has weakened the Zenoth's magicks. They are forced to watch as the Fae fall in droves to Mezilmoth's corrupted army. Those who serve the light are on the run, fleeing to the last stronghold in Zenafrost: the home of the Forest Dwellers. The mountains that cut through the countryside stand resolute in their way. With Mezilmoth closing in from behind, the Zenoths usher the Fae up the steep rocks, their path led by Velisa and Ingard. The Zenoths stay at the foot of the mountain, determined to safeguard their beloved Fae with all they are, to combine their dwindling powers to slow their brother's advance. They will do what they must to protect that which they created so long ago.

The hands of fate inch ever closer, reaching towards the inevitable.

CHAPTER 7

THE MAKING OF A LEGEND

Their screams...Ax was certain he'd never be rid of them. How long had it been since this war began? Since Mezilmoth had fallen and damned them all? At first, he thought the steady decline of his powers would be the worst of it. For surely he and his brethren would still be enough to stop whatever plan Mezilmoth could concoct. But that idea faded quickly into fancy. It was clear from the very beginning, from the first battle waged: they were outmatched by the darkness.

Mezilmoth had taken to the land like a shadow. His presence stilled the clouds, blackened the air, and sucked the life from the earth. All he touched fell to his corruption. The whispering woods now spoke in nightmarish tongue, driving those who heard it mad. The fertile soil was poisoned, seeping into the crops and streams. And the people who called Zenafrost home...well, they got the worst of it. Ax had seen so many men and women changed by the dark magicks. Tainted, torn, built again in his vision. A vision of death. They served him blindly, killing and taking any that stood against them. It was their screams that haunted him.

He had spent the entirety of the war on the front lines. Though the Zenoths powers were fading, his knowledge of the healing arts made him indispensable. The magick that imbued the Fae seemed unaffected by the fall of the Chamber, though it did little against the wrath of Mezilmoth. While Ingard and Ax tried to save as many of the injured warriors as they could, Velisa assisted Bardro and the Zenoths in the depths of combat. At times, it had seemed like they stood a chance.

This futile hope was all that drove them onward.

Now here they stood once more. The Fae's cries of agony had vanished on the wind, carried up the mountain with their departure. Ax hadn't the heart to tell Velisa and Ingard goodbye. To speak the words would make it true, and the heartbreak of never seeing them again was something Ax knew would end him. They had instead left with a hug, and the whispered words "Be safe," choked from his throat.

The Zenoths stood side by side, a wall of magick and dimming cosmic power. Ax had never seen his bloodlings so tired, so weary, so broken. What was to come need not be said, for they all knew what this likely meant. The decision to remain here, to meet Mezilmoth's army and give the Fae as much of a head start as they could, would be their last.

Nora and Bardro stood in the center of their line. The eldest, and their leaders in this war to save all. Before every battle, Bardro had taken to giving great speeches. He would stand before the legions of Fae and Zenoths, rallying them with his mighty words and powerful, infectious energy. He, above all others, believed that light could still win against the darkness. Ax admired him deeply for this. He strived to believe the same, even as the hope died in his heart with every passing battle.

But this time was different. Bardro did not step before them as clear leader, building them up for the coming attack. Instead, he stayed beside them, facing the fog that shrouded the land. Their equal.

Friya shuddered beside Ax. "They're coming," she said, breaking the aching silence.

Ax strained his ears to listen. He could hear no movement, no approach on the horizon. But he could feel it all the same. The sudden shift in the air, growing still against them. The pricking of dark energy across his skin, setting his teeth on edge. The fog had begun to move, like shadows in the night.

"Hold fast," Bardro said. The command in his voice steadied Ax's uneven heartbeat.

They watched as shapes appeared in the fog. Giant, nightmarish figures painted black against the shroud; they were there one second, gone the next. The suspense and unease rippled through the Zenoths, wavering the group's resolve.

"Enough of this," Nora growled, a tone Ax had never heard her use. Her eyes glowed white, and she shot a beam of blinding light across the edge of the fog. It dispersed in an instant, casting into frightening relief the horrors that stood before them.

They numbered in the thousands. Terrifying beasts of all shapes and sizes. Some still seemed trapped between man and monster, features of the Fae they once were clinging to the corruption. Others were long gone, sprouting clawing limbs and gnashing maws that sought blood and bone. Ax could see fresh flesh stuck between the teeth of many of the monsters closest. His blood ran cold.

Amongst these lesser beasts stood Mezilmoth's greatest creations. Seven Fae with extraordinary powers whom he took and transformed into his own. On the battlefield, Ax had heard them called 'the Prime Corruptions.' Their dark magick outweighed any single warrior or Zenoth, and none had yet fallen in the war. They were most horrific of all, the closest one wearing armor made from the sharpened bones of fallen Fae children. His pulsating green eyes fell on Ax, his face splitting into a smile that cut his head clean in two. Inside his mouth were rows and rows of razor-sharp teeth, and Ax could see a hand still sliding down his throat to his stomach.

Leading the hoard, the face of evil itself, was Mezilmoth. He wore black robes that faded into shadow beneath him. Ax knew these shadows could move of their own accord, as he had watched them kill many who had attempted to end Mezilmoth themselves. The robes were as grand as any king's, leading up to a high collar that shrouded the bottom half of his face. The top half was unnaturally pale, like bone that had been dusted in starlight. His red streaked eyes were the most vicious shade of green, reminding Ax of a poisonous plant. Black hair billowed out around him, blending in with the fabric of his robes. Light crackled like broken stone at the tips of his blood-stained fingers.

He cocked his head at Nora, raising a brow at the light still pulsing in her palms. "Now, sister," he crooned. "Is that anyway to greet me?" He waved his hand idly, and the light vanished from Nora's grip.

Ax's heart dropped. Mezilmoth had done nothing but grow in power, even as their own faltered. There was no telling the extent of his magick now. This did not bode well.

"Traitor," Friya hissed. "You have defiled all that is, was, and ever will be!"

Mezilmoth gave a dramatic gasp, his hand fluttering to his heart. "Defiled? My darling Friya, I'm hurt! Why, I've done nothing but strengthen magick, since it was placed in my care. The great crystal was meaningless compared to what I now possess. Tell me, how is *your* magicks these days?" A smile curved on his face, and laughter echoed from the hordes of darkness. It was a cruel, thrashing sound.

Ax was infuriated. "You're *killing* those we bore into this universe! Those we swore to protect!" he cried.

Mezilmoth looked around him, making a grand motion with his arms. The smile was still set on his face as he turned back to Ax. "I *have* protected them. I protect all those who follow me, brother. And it seems to me that it is *you* who falls short of your promise. Perhaps if you were stronger, you would have stood a chance against me. Against the inevitable."

Ax opened his mouth to speak, but found words failed him.

"There is no use speaking to him," Bardro said. He was looking at Mezilmoth in cold disgust. "Reason left him when he fell to the darkness."

Mezilmoth hissed suddenly at Bardro, the sound echoed by the black beasts around him. "Do not speak to me of reason, Bardro. It is 'reason' that has led you to this war. I wanted you to join me, to stand with me in aligning the cosmos as they are meant to be. It was you who chose this path of ruin and bloodshed. You and your blind servitude to the light." He spat on the earth, and the ground it struck sizzled like acid rain. "There is no 'reason.' There is only power, and those brave enough to seize it."

And without warning, the dark army attacked.

Ax barely had time to move. He raised his hands, crying out. A shield appeared around himself and Friya, extending slowly out across the line of Zenoths. Flashes of light collided with bolts of darkness. The sound was like breaking earth and thunder. Lightning struck from the sky. Shadows pressed against Ax's shield. Friya threw chunks of sharpened boulders at the descending monsters. A ways ahead, Bardro wielded a sword of light. He was locked in fierce battle with the shadows that surrounded Mezilmoth. His blade cut through their darkness, dripping black ooze onto the soil like blood.

Tapping into his fury, Ax brought his hands high. A battle cry ripped from him. Blue magick crackled to life in his hands. In response, giant pillars of vibrant lighting shot from the clouds. They struck the earth with earsplitting sound, felling great chunks of monsters as they came. Nora looked like the sun, chasing back the shadows with her rays of light. Ax could hear screams amidst his bloodlings. He could spare no time to see who was falling among them.

Friya let out a gasp, her attacks ceasing. Ax's magick waivered, distracted by what he knew was her all-seeing eye. She shook herself free from her vision, then turned with a face twisted in horror. Her hand stretched past Ax as she cried, "*Bardro!*"

Time seemed to slow. Ax spun to face his brother. Bardro had driven back Mezilmoth's shadows for a moment, his sword held high above his head. It pointed towards the sky like a conduit of light. Bardro locked eyes with Ax, and gave him a rare, soft smile. And it became clear what he meant to do.

"NO!" Ax screamed, abandoning his shield and the lighting strikes. He made to move towards Bardro, but it was already too late. A beam of light shot from Bardro's sword and into the sky. Tethers of this same light appeared around Ax, Friya, Nora, and all the remaining Zenoths. They were hoisted into the sky, pulled against their will to far above the battle. Ax thrashed against the binds, but it was useless. He screamed, reaching towards the ground where his brother now stood, alone before the darkness.

CHAPTER 8
BARDRO

Ax's screams of anguish echoed in Bardro's head. It took all his might not to look up to him in comfort. With the remnants of his magick, he had done two things. First, he had removed his family from harm's way. Two, he had sent out a final signal, calling out for one who owed him his life. He prayed it would be worth it. For he now stood before his brother, his eldest brother whom he once idolized so, with nothing to protect him.

He drove his sword into the earth, assuring that the tethers of light would remain until help arrived. That his family would hopefully be spared. As the sword sunk into the ground, Bardro felt something strike him in the chest. It winded him, throwing him careening back into the mountainside. Wet warmth pooled beneath the spot where he laid, and though he could not feel it, he knew he was mortally wounded.

A tendril of shadow appeared around his wrist, a second entwining around the other. He was lifted by his arms into the air, and slammed hard against the rock face behind him. He sputtered at the impact, and saw blood fly from his mouth. The dark magick felt like tiny blades against his skin, burning into his flesh. His ears rang with the sound of Ax's screaming.

Mezilmoth approached him, his beasts and monsters parting like the tide as he moved. Another tendril of smoke made its way up Ax's body, wrapping slowly around his neck. Mezilmoth stopped inches away from him, glancing up towards their suspended siblings in the sky. "You have made them into live bait for my creations," he said, clearly amused. "And given yourself to me as a lamb to slaughter. I fail to see your motivations." He drew a finger across Bardro's cheek, a seemingly tender motion that left a streak of burned skin in its wake.

"I'm sorry, brother," Bardro said in a strangled voice, fighting to breathe against the tendril of shadow. "You taught us so much, and yet we failed to teach you what it means to be good. What it means to love. I am so sorry."

Mezilmoth paused, his finger still trailing down Bardro's cheek. His cool visage cracked, a ripple of rage flashing across it. He leaned even closer to Bardro's face, studying his eyes. "You know, brother...I always did hate how insistent you were on having the final word."

And with a flick of his hand, he severed Bardro's tongue in his mouth.

White-hot pain ripped through him, but he refused to give him the satisfaction of a scream. He spit his tongue to the ground, blood pouring from his mouth. Mezilmoth placed his hand against Bardro's chest, his eyes suddenly glowing. Darkness began to pulse from his palms and into Bardro's body. He was trying to corrupt him, to add him to his dark army and use him as a weapon against his family.

Bardro shut his eyes, zeroing in on the overwhelming tide of darkness within him. He could feel how tainted it was, feel how it had already begun to twist his insides. But beneath the shadows, the core magic did not feel so different from his own. He gripped on to this feeling, holding it with all he was. With every last bit of his strength, he forced his pinned arms downwards, slamming his palms against the face of the mountain. Down, down, down he pushed the magick: through his chest, down his arms, to his hands. His eyes flew open to find Mezilmoth, looking shocked and confused. He had a second's control over Mezilmoth's power. And Bardro flashed him a bloody grin before shooting every bit of that harnessed magick into the mountain behind him.

There was an explosion that blasted Mezilmoth clear away from Bardro, throwing him back into the forces of darkness. Magick erupted from the back of Bardro, cracking into the mountain with a mix of light and dark veins. There was a world-shaking *boom*, and the mountain split clean around Bardro. The tendrils of shadows vanished, dropping him to the ground. And through the settling dust of the freshly made pass in the mountain, a great shadow swept forth. Breathing was becoming near impossible as Bardro lay there, but he smiled still. His final act had worked.

The dragon had come.

CHAPTER 9
AX

Ax shrieked as Bardro's body dropped, the sound repeated by his bloodlings. Nora was firing beam after beam of sunlight towards the earth, desperately trying to strike Mezilmoth where he lay, stunned. They watched as the mountain split almost perfectly in two. And something swept out from the pass it created.

The dust was blasted aside by the beating of great wings, and a dragon was suddenly standing beside Bardro. It bent its huge head down towards their fallen brother, closing its dazzling eyes. Smoke trailed from its nostrils, and Ax felt as if it were saying something to Bardro. And when it rose again, it was with an air of unending wrath. It roared, the sound shaking more rocks loose from the still-settling mountain. It spread its wings wide and took to the sky, angling down towards Mezilmoth's army.

A wall of fire shot from its mouth. It engulfed the dark forces in brilliant golden flame, covering them in an instant. It swept back and forth above them, blanketing them in unending attack. Ax could see Mezilmoth enshrouded in a shield of dark magick, protecting himself. But they were all turning, turning away from the mountain as they fled the relentless barrage of the dragon. And as they began to vanish into the distance, the great tendrils of light finally began to waiver and lowered the Zenoths to the ground.

Ax was the first to Bardro's side, falling on his knees beside his brother as the rest struggled to keep up. Bardro's body had been broken, nearly every bone shattered within him. His flesh looked rotted around the area Mezilmoth had touched, a great purple band across his throat. Blood leaked from his eyes, his ears, his mouth.

Ax could hardly see through his tears. Hardly felt when his bloodlings fell to their knees around him, Nora right at his side. He lifted Bardro's head gingerly into his arms. "No," he sobbed. "No, no, no. Please, you can't go. You mustn't. I can't..."

Bardro looked up at Ax, tears mixing with the blood on his beaten face. He let out a strange noise, somewhere between a gurgle and a comforting shush. Then his eyes slid from Ax's face, staring off into the clouds above them. The beam of light, still radiating from his sword, extinguished. And the life left his gaze.

Ax shook him gently. "No, please!" he cried, his tears now falling onto his face as well. "Bardro! Please, don't leave us!" But even as he held him, Bardro's body began to change, reverting to the cosmic ash from which all Zenoths are born. Ax tried to tighten his grip as his brother's skin began to turn to stardust in his hands. The wind was swirling in strange patterns around them, seeming to whisper as it passed.

"Shh," Ax heard softly in his ear. Like an echo of his brother's voice. "Shh." The wind spun around the pile of stardust in Ax's lap. It whisked it up in one gust, creating a glimmering ball of light above them. Then it left with the remains of him, rocketing towards what looked to be the shoreline in the distance.

Ax continued to weep, Nora holding him tight. The Zenoths cried together, for the loss of their brother, and the loss of all their hope. They wept for what felt like hours, sitting in the rubble and ruin of the battle and this desperate sacrifice. They only paused when the great gusts of wind came, and the dragon landed amongst them once more.

It towered over them, but Ax couldn't bring himself to look up from where Bardro has once lay.

"You came for my brother," Nora said, in more of a statement than a question. "Why?"

Ax was startled when the dragon spoke, its voice booming. "Your brother saved my life once, long ago. My debt to him has been paid in kind."

"Please," Ax said, in a voice barely above a whisper. "Please, you must help us." He looked up at the dragon, anguish ripping through him. "He sacrificed his life to bring you here. We need you, if we are to have even the dimmest hope of sealing Mezilmoth away."

The dragon stared at him with deeply appraising eyes. "My debt was to your brother, and as I said: it has been paid." He paused, looking around at the wreckage left behind by the dark army. "However...it seems his favor may have extended beyond simply delaying their assault. Far beyond. Very well, little one. I will remain to help you see the end of the battle your brother led." It bowed low to the Zenoths, his wings sweeping across the ground.

Ax rose slowly from the earth, bits of stardust still clinging to his clammy skin. He stared off towards the shoreline, where the waves seemed to have ripped up into a desperate frenzy. He could feel the terror and shock of his bloodlings, still sniffling and stunned around him. He took a deep breath, and asked himself, '*What would my brother do?*'

He turned to face them all, glancing at the look of dim admiration on Nora's tear-stained face. "We've got one final shot at this thing. One last chance to stop him. We know he's bent on killing us off before he finishes the Fae. He's made that clear enough. So, we'll use it to our advantage. We'll lead him as far towards the edge of Zenafrost as we can, raise the earth so high there that none could ever hope of touching it. And with the last of our magick, we will tear a hole in the cosmos and seal him away inside."

They continued to stare at him, with varying looks of fear and pain. He gulped back the next wave of tears that threatened to overtake him. There would be time to mourn. But now was the time for action. "Bardro laid this plan for us. Sacrificed...sacrificed himself for the Fae. And for us. We will not ... no. *I cannot* fail him."

Nora placed a hand on his shoulder. "We stand with you, my brother. And with Bardro."

"We all do," one of the other Zenoths added to the nods of the rest.

"Then let us end it," Ax said, turning from the place his brother had fallen and leading them into the gash through the mountain.

The fate of all hangs in the balance.

The blackened skies cast shadows over every inch of the world. The wind carries the screams of the fallen in a seemingly endless echo. As the Fae flee for the safety of the Forest Dwellers home, the last of the Zenoths bait Mezilmoth and his army to the edge of Zenafrost. There is only one hope that remains, only one thing that could possibly stop the beginning of the end.

But magick powerful enough to rip a whole through the fabric of the universe must always come with a price.

Axoliphim

CHAPTER 10

IN THE END OF ALL THINGS

It is a mighty thing, to lose so much. I had experienced it before but nothing like this. I had no time, no moment to breathe between each fallen friend. It felt like a dream, one which had no beginning and no end. My heart had been left on one of the first battlefields, left with the ashes and the blood and the agony. And I was sure I would never get it back. Most especially not now. Whatever hope had remained of that surely was laid to rest with Bardro's broken body at the foot of the mountains.

And so, I ran with my bloodlings. We ran through the pass, flanked by the wind off the wings of the great dragon. Down hillsides once so green, now laid barren by the darkness and death. We crossed the valley where magick had no place, a valley where Zenafrost disallowed us to use that which had given her life. And I could feel her pain beneath my feet. It flowed through the earth like a plague, crying, begging for help. For justice.

We never once stopped on that trek. By the clouds in the skies, we could tell Mezilmoth was never far behind. I could feel him approaching, like sickness against my cold skin. All I could do was pray, pray to the universe and Beyonds that the Fae were safe. That my friends, my family...that they would remember us.

For I felt almost certain few of us would survive.

Though our journey felt like ages, it seemed that in the blink of an eye we now stood on the very edge of Zenafrost. The little of us left huddled on the cliffside, staring out across the waters below. They were angry, much angrier than they'd ever been before. The waves slammed into the rockface, and the wind shot by so quickly, it stung my cheeks. Behind us, a black mist was approaching, gaining in speed and ferocity, impossible to see through.

This was it.

Our plan was simple: lure Mezilmoth onto the plains with his great army, then we would use our combined magicks to raise the plateau far, far into the skies. When we were well away from the fragile earth below, we would tear through the universe, using the last our powers to create a hole into the End of All Things. This was a realm of dark nothingness; a place where nothing could exist. And it was here we would seal our brother away, to never cause harm to another. A feat that was much easier spoken than done.

I was so focused on the plan, and on the approaching dark magick ahead, that I nearly missed the sound that came next; the sound of approaching hoofbeats to the south. My eyes flew to the source, only to have all breath leave my body.

Silhouetted by the little sun that remained above the southern forest, riding atop galloping creatures of flora and wood, were the Fae warriors. Those who had taken the gift of magick, those that still remained of the forces that fought alongside of us, had left the safety of the Forest Dweller's magick to join us once more. And at the head, leading them onward with swords of glowing gold and blue magick, were Ingard and Velisa. I felt guilty for the pride and joy that rocketed through me to see their faces again.

They came to a halt before us, dismounting their beautiful steeds in a clatter of armor and weaponry. I stared open-mouthed as Velisa and Ingard approached. For what could I hope to say in these final moments?

But Velisa took my hand steadfast in hers. And she smiled wide at me, as if the world was not rested haphazardly on our backs. "You didn't truly think we'd let you go at it alone, did you, Ax?"

Ingard patted one of his impossibly large hands on my shoulder, and I could feel the electric current of his magick whizzing through me. "The Fae are safe within the forest borders. What you see here," he motioned wide at the Fae forces taking their places amongst the Zenoths, "are those who demanded to join us at arms."

"You don't understand," I managed to breathe. I had been wrong before. My heart was surely still with me and threatening to plummet from my chest with their arrival. "You must escape while you still have time-"

Velisa squeezed my hand tighter. It was so warm, so strange when the air all around had grown icy cold. "You'll not be rid of us. Not ever. So, tell us what we are to do."

I stammered only a moment longer before catching myself finally. There was no use. There was no time for them to turn back now, and no sense in arguing the point. I explained the plan to them, just as quickly as I could. The great dragon was taking his position before us, facing towards the approaching army. It was all happening so fast. A whisper of fear overtook our small army.

"My family." It was Nora, striding to the forefront of the crowd with her hands held before her. Our forces grew silent as she spoke. She looked so odd, standing there in full armor. So far from the sister with flowers in her hair and trinkets made by Fae children adorning her person. Even the wind seemed to lay still as she went on. "We stand now at the precipice of good and evil. We are the last stronghold against what would be the death of all light in the universe. We have all lost so, so much...so many of our loved ones have stood against this tide of destruction. Have been a shield to our home. And it is up to us now, to make sure their departure to the Beyonds is not in vain."

Ingard came to stand alongside her now, his great axe crackling with bolts of golden lightning. He flashed his smile, that looked like the stars themselves had crafted it. "Aye, lads. Thousands of years we've had on this earth. Thousands of years together, perfecting our magicks and living our beautiful lives. Are we gonna let this bastard sweep through and destroy everything we've created?!"

A great "NO!" echoed out in unison, from both Fae and Zenoth alike.

"Then stand true and firm! And let's show the darkness that it stands no more chance against our light!"

I joined in the battle cry that was released from our army. It was bittersweet. Though we were prepared to stand and fight, I could see the thought behind the eyes of all: few if any would leave this last battle alive. On both sides. But once again, there was no time to entertain such things. Mezilmoth was upon us, stepping past the boundary line we had decided upon.

Nora turned her back to our forces, who had gathered in true formation behind her. I took my place in line alongside Velisa, her hands full of sunbeams. I stood staring at the backs of Nora and Ingard. Nora's entire body had become shrouded in her sunlit magick, mirroring Velisa. Ingard was like a storm cloud, lightning lacing through the joints of his armor and up his battle axe. It reminded me of standing behind Nora and Bardro. And I felt my heart break anew. I released the rest of my magick, and the skies above cracked blue with the thunder of my pain.

As planned, the great dragon swept suddenly into the skies. His wings sent great torrents of wind across the plains, clearing the magicked mist from around Mezilmoth's army. And Beyonds Be, what an army it was. It seemed no matter how many of his forces we fell, he would merely raise them back to fight alongside him once more. With the mists gone, we could hear them now: screaming, roaring, snarling and spitting. It was a sea of ooze dotted with nightmarish faces. The sight made my skin crawl.

From above, the dragon let out a great roar and shot fire down around the dark army. They were trapped momentarily, surrounded by the wall of dragon's fire. I couldn't see where Mezilmoth was through the torrent of flame and darkness, but I could feel his overwhelming magick somewhere within the crowd. So, we took what little time we had.

In unison, the Zenoths raised their hands high. The Fae were battle ready, their own magicks now more powerful than ours alone. I could see stone rising into the air around some, root and vine coming to life by the beckoning of others. It never ceased to be beautiful, seeing my bloodlings' magick brought to life by the Fae they had been gifted to. I fell to my knees with the other Zenoths, slamming our hands into the earth and concentrating all I was into my palms.

The ground began to tremble and shake. A noise like a great, low groan cracked through the air, and the earth began to rise. We broke free of the plains, rocketing a great mass of the continent into the sky and creating the highest cliff I'd ever seen. I could feel it draining me, the force it took to change the earth. Even with the help of my bloodlings. By the time we reached high enough to stop, I feared about my ability to fight, let alone tear open a doorway through the universe itself.

As the earth stopped moving, there was a tremendous clap of energy from the other side of the flaming wall. With a torrent of wind that knocked some of the standing Fae to their knees alongside of us, the fire vanished. And I was suddenly staring at the face of Mezilmoth.

He looked nothing like my brother, all remnant of that beautiful magickal being gone. His skin was sallow, sickly. It stretched across his body as if it were not his own. As if he were wearing someone else's. The bones beneath looked strangely jagged and sharp, poking through in some places and leaving great red and purple bruises in others. Even from his distance, I could see his eyes. Black as starless skies and swimming in what looked to be the ooze that came from many of his dark creations. He was shrouded in a cloak made of the hide of a Fury. The fur had been stained red in places by sprays of blood. And when he smiled at me, it revealed far too many teeth in his animal-like mouth.

I felt nothing but pure, white-hot rage. And it was I who shot the first attack at this monster who wore my brother's face.

CRACK.

Lightning descended from above the army, far more than I had conjured. I realized that Ingard had fired away in tandem with me, supercharging my magick as his joined with mine. The flash blinded me momentarily, sending the dark army scattering. Mezilmoth did not move, and even though the bolt was powerful enough to shake the whole of the plateau, he deflected it with ease. It flew into a chunk of his forces, exploding them on impact. But he was unperturbed.

The forces gathered themselves again, then launched forward towards us. And as a handful of us turned to rip open the fabric of the world, the Fae raised their arms and rushed to meet them. Those not opening the portal joined the Fae army, and chaos erupted. The dragon sent wave after wave of fire upon Mezilmoth's army, but only dented the forces as he set the world ablaze. As I ran towards the cliffside with Nora, Friya and Ilfred, I glanced over my shoulder.

Magick shot from both sides, in shades of gold and blue and green and red and black. Rocks and stone, chunks of earth and bits of sky all flew about, striking down dark and light alike. I tried to block out the screams that had already started across the plateau. And there, moving slowly towards us through the battle, was Mezilmoth. Though bolts of magick aimed to strike him, he remained entirely untouched.

"Hurry!" Friya cried from beside me. "We must hurry!"

We hit the edge of the cliff and came to a halt. Each of us placed a hand on Nora's back, joining our magick cores as she reached out into the air before us. The pull of energy that began was massive, like a blackhole in the world, begging to suck us all in. A pinprick of impossible darkness appeared before us. Nora clutched her hands into fists, as if grabbing this pinprick, and she began to pull her hands away from one another.

It was painfully, impossibly slow. I could feel the amount of magick we were expending. It sucked the life from me, tugging at my soul as Nora used all that we were to tear into the world. The clatter of battle was approaching us from behind. The screams of the falling warriors ached in my ears. But I could not pull away. This was our only chance, our only hope. I could feel Mezilmoth getting closer and closer, feel his darkness threatening to consume us all.

Beside me, my brother Ilfred released his hold on Nora. The tiny portal before us slowed even further, but the remaining three of us held fast. I followed him with my eyes, watching his hands light up with the starlit magick he possessed. Mezilmoth was yards away, his head cocked to the side as he stopped to watch Ilfred.

What looked like shooting stars burst forth from Ilfred's hands, flying at our brother with unprecedented force. I was shocked out how much power he was still able to expel, when I myself felt like my entire being was going to be used to open this rift. They struck the impenetrable shield around Mezilmoth, sending veins of stardust across it. Then Mezilmoth raised his hand and gave a flourish.

Ilfred grabbed at his throat, gasping and sputtering. Friya began to sob, but none of us removed our hands from Nora. Ilfred's face was turning red, purple, blue. Then with a sickening *pop,* his head exploded.

Friya and I cried out in unison. The portal, just large enough to fit a child through now, shuddered and paused before Nora continued to wrench it open. Lightning cracked at the sky, from me or Ingard battling behind me, I did not know. Friya let out a sudden gasp beside me, a noise I knew all too well. My eyes widened as I turned to look at her, the portal now large enough to force a fully grown person through. Mezilmoth was feet away, and I could see him smiling wickedly out of the corner of my eye. But there was nothing any of us could do about what came next.

Friya was having a vision. One so powerful, it froze every being on the plateau around us where they stood. Even the mighty dragon approaching from above hung suspended, all noise vanishing save for the whipping wind now raising Friya slowly into the air. Her eyes were entirely white, her hands held out to her sides and hair whipping across her emotionless face. And when she spoke, it was in a voice that came from everywhere and echoed for what I was sure was miles all around.

"When time has passed, and earth lay black.
When air chokes thick from corruption's crack.
When darkness wins over sealed gate,
And the end of all is only fate.
Only then can life be saved
By starlit will and determined brave.
Sealed back by dawn and light
The blood of the one to end all plight."

TIME BEGAN ANEW, and many things happened as one. As the deafening roar of battle kicked up, Nora and I stepped back from the gate. Friya hit the ground as Mezilmoth roared, sending a wave of dark magick straight for her. I dove for my sister, but the shot was too quick. The darkness struck Friya in the chest, and with a shuddering gasp, my sister erupted into ash.

I shrieked as Nora and I fell to our knees where she had just stood, holding the ashes now scattering in the wind to my chest. Then Mezilmoth was screaming, drawing our attention back to the place where he stood.

Mezilmoth's shield had momentarily dissipated with the freeze of Friya's prophecy. And in this moment, Velisa had sprung up behind him. Her hand was driven deep into his back, her face set in a mask of resolute vengeance as she roared in time with his shrieking.

"Velisa, NO!" I could see what was coming. I knew, before I could even lunge towards them. They were too far away. My hands were outstretched, but I had no magick left to give. Velisa's magick was cracking golden veins through the darkness that was Mezilmoth. The darkness of his eyes became laced with sunlight. And as black ooze spewed from his mouth, he launched spikes of bones from his body.

And I watched as Velisa was impaled against him.

My screams tangled with two more, Nora and Ingard joining me. A pillar of lightning struck Mezilmoth, forcing him to retract his spikes and stumble forward towards the portal behind us.

I forgot about the battle. My ears were deaf to the sounds around us. I caught Velisa as she fell to the earth, holding her against my chest. Ingard fell beside us, and together we held Velisa bleeding in our arms. She smiled as she looked up at us, her teeth red with blood as it pooled in her mouth. Her chest lay open, a gaping hole clean through her.

"Velisa," Ingard breathed, with such pain as I had never heard. Like his soul was dying with her.

"You're okay," I heard myself repeating. "I've got you, it's gonna be okay." My hands fumbled helplessly at her chest, trying desperately to heal a wound that I knew could not be changed. "Stay with me, Vel. You're going to be okay, you just...you just have to stay."

A hand fluttered to my cheek. All her previous warmth was gone. The coldness of her skin wrenched a sob from me. She smiled again, squeezing Ingard's hand as she caressed my cheek one last time. And with a gurgled sort of laugh, she spoke to me the first words I ever said to her. "Be not afraid, starling." Then her eyes dimmed. And Velisa was gone.

Ingard was weeping, the ground around him cracking as bolts of electricity shot through the earth from his body. He lifted her out of my lap and into his arms, cradling her against him as he rocked gently. The sound of battle came into relief once more. And I was filled with a hatred unrivaled.

I rose from my place beside Ingard, turning slowly with blind fury to the place where Nora still stood. She was engaged in battle with a heavily injured Mezilmoth, firing an endless beam of sunlit magick into his chest while deflecting the darkness he sent her way. The dragon above us was beating his wings furiously, sending Mezilmoth back through the dirt, inching towards the rift.

I gripped to the wrath and fury, to my pain and my desperation. I raised my hands, soaked in the blood of my best friend, of the one who had taught me so, so much. And with every last bit of who I was, I shot a pillar of white lighting into Mezilmoth.

My magick joined with Nora's, looping with her sunlight in a strange dance. There was a sound like the chiming of bells, our joined beam of magick exploding smalls bursts of sparks from itself as it forced the roaring Mezilmoth back, back, back. And together with the dragon's wind, we threw Mezilmoth into the impenetrable darkness beyond the rift.

As soon as the magick ceased, I collapsed to the ground. I had nothing left. I half prayed this would be the end, that I would close my eyes and wake up in the Beyonds beside Velisa. I could feel consciousness slipping away. Nora was crying out for me, and I tried to lift myself from the earth. But it was no use. My arms and legs did not move as I forced my eyes to open.

Tendrils of darkness were reaching out towards us from within the rift. They burned and singed the ground as they went, weaving up and around the edges of the portal to hold it open. Nora was standing before it, her glowing golden magick wavering as she tried to keep our brother from escaping. I fought desperately to stand, but it was all I could do to remain conscious. Someone was placing a hand on my head, leaning down towards my ear.

"Keep them safe, will you friend?" Ingard had risen from Velisa's body, coming to kneel beside me. He stood and strode towards Nora, whose eyes were brimmed in tears. She stretched her hand out to him, and I saw him smile at her as he took it.

They stood hand in hand together, the joining of their gold and blue magick erupting in the same chiming sound as before. The world was starting to dim, my mind trying desperately to escape the pain and the exhaustion. But I forced myself to remain. Forced myself to bear witness to this one final act of love by my sister, and my brother.

The darkness struck against their magick again and again, but it held like a great shimmering shield, protecting our world from what would have been the end. The shield of magick was overtaking Nora and Ingard, hardening them into what looked like carved marble as they stood unmoving before the darkness. And when it ceased, all that remained was a great circular gate, suspended at the edge of the cliffside. An eerie silence fell as I stared at the carved forms of Nora and Ingard, hands still clasped, and arms raised before them, frozen as the last line of defense for our universe.

The tears fell from my eyes as they closed. And I was thrown into the cold stillness of unconsciousness.

The battle for Zenafrost is over. It has been won, but at a fatal cost to all those who were present.

There is no celebration, no victory amongst the dead.

The Fae have split into factions, rebuilding their homesteads in the corners of the world. The Zenoths, along with some of the Fae, cannot bear to remain in the place where so many of their loved ones were lost. They have chosen to leave their world, travelling through a rift in the cosmos on a far-flung island.

But there is one that chooses to stay. To remain as a watchful eye over the Fae and the home they so loved.

CHAPTER II

EXODUS

The time after the war passed in a haze of buried friends and rain-washed blood stains. The memory of those lost lived on only in those who had survived. The remaining Zenoths, distraught by what one of their own had wrought upon their homes, could not bring themselves to walk her earths any longer. Alongside many Fae who shared this heartbreak, they planned to make an exodus from Zenafrost.

Forever.

Days before this great leaving, one of the eldest remaining Zenoths walked with labored pace across the freshly cleaned pastures of the eastern wood. Riamore moved with deliberate slowness, out of both awkwardness for his task, and respect for what he knew he was walking into. The Library of Time, well-kept even during the war, was showing signs of decay beyond its age. The once clear crystal of the great tower had begun to turn grey, cracking with smoke-like constellations. Dark plumes of ivy creeped up around it; earthen fingers begging to reclaim this ancient place for its own. The energy was thick in a way Riamore did not recognize. This was something new. Something aching.

He felt nearly strangled by it as he walked through the threshold, moving towards the innermost chamber of the library. He noted the array of books that looked to have been blasted from the shelves. Pages littered every inch of floor, bits of wall and roof falling away in places. Birds had taken up residency in many of the rooms he passed, chittering away at him as he disrupted their immense quiet.

Riamore slowed his pace even further as he approached the inner chamber. He could see his brother, sitting in the same place he had been nearly every day for a full moon cycle. Positioned by the largest window, sitting on a poof that was much too small for his frame, was Axoliphim. His hair was ragged about him, longer than Riamore had ever seen. He had a long, trailing beard to match, draped across his dark blue robes which served as his only covering. There was a small leather-bound journal clasped in one of his pale hands, the other trailing a finger gently across the great stretches of burnt wall beside him.

"Brother," Riamore said softly when he had made it to his side. "It is nearly time."

Axoliphim stopped moving, freezing in place like a perfect statue. Riamore mimicked the motion, feeling the cold air that swept across the room. It had been this way every time Riamore had visited since the war. Of all the Zenoths and Fae, of all those lost and all things witnessed, Ax was perhaps the most devastating surviving casualty of the war. He had been pulled from the freshly made Outer Plain, sobbing, shrieking, and nearly taking out the entire plateau as he went. When they had found him, he was cradling Velisa's cold corpse, silent and unmoving as he sat with his back to the Dark Gate. A gate which held two carvings of both his sister and his dear friend.

He had not been the same since.

When he returned to the tower, the shockwaves of his tumultuous heartbreak could be felt throughout much of the land. And when the silence finally fell, the Zenoths entered to find him exactly as he was now: silent and unmoving.

Riamore fidgeted nervously. "The others...Axoliphim, our bloodlings worry for you. *I* worry for you. This misery you have made home in will be the death of you. It brings with it a darkness that we fear may change you."

"Change me." It was the first time Riamore had heard him speak since the war. His voice was haggard, cracking, and worn. Lightning sparked at his fingertips. Riamore took a step back on instinct. "Is that what this is then, brother? You have all grown to fear me?"

Riamore fidgeted again, eyes flicking down to the lightning lacing through Ax's fingers. "We are worried only by what you may become. After what we've all just seen-

"Do you mean to enter my chamber and compare me to Mezilmoth, Riamore?"

The cold chill swept through once more. Riamore shivered against it. "Not to compare you. No."

Ax suddenly moved his gaze to Riamore. His eyes were steel; lifeless and shadowed by a pain that no words could bring meaning to. That perhaps nothing could heal. It took every ounce of willpower in Riamore to not look away from such a stare.

"I have no intention of leaving my home," Ax said in a voice barely above a whisper. "I will not turn tail and run from that which we have created. I will not leave them defenseless."

"Defenseless?" Riamore replied, kneeling beside Ax. "Brother, you of all people know that the threat was ended. He was sealed away behind the Dark Gate-"

"Do not speak that name to me," Ax snapped, redrawing his eyes to stare pointedly out the window.

Riamore bowed his head. "You must understand, Ax. We are *all* concerned for the Fae that have chosen to remain. We wonder if more threats will come, but what brought *this* threat...it was us." He let out a sad sigh. "We cannot, in good conscious, remain when one of our own has spilled so much innocent blood."

Ax let out a humorless laugh. "Ah, to be unburdened by that which you have created. What must that be like, I wonder?"

There was sullen silence, Riamore rising back to his feet as if he had been spat upon. He stared out the window with Ax, towards a garden that had once been tended by Velisa, held safe by the magick she had imbued into the land there. Riamore's heart broke ever further for his brother. "Many of our bloodlings worry for this path you are on," he repeated.

"Yes, we've established you are all afraid of me."

Riamore tsked. "As I said, we too worry for the fate of these lands. And leaving one of us behind, particularly one in your delicate state-"

Ax was on his feet in an instant. The room, which had seconds ago been filled with dusty sunlight, was now the pitch black of the mightiest storms. Riamore was dwarfed by the size Axoliphim was becoming, shedding his earthly skin, and exposing his cosmic form. It was a beautiful and terrifying sight to behold.

Thunder shook the room, lightning crashed through bookshelves and erupted from Ax's eyes like star fall. "You call me delicate while shrieking of your blind fears? All to flee from a land that has never needed us more? You are *cowards*. I would rather *die* than leave what Nora worked so hard to create. What they have *all* worked so hard to create." He was shrinking back to his normal size now, looking exhausted as the light pooled back into the room.

Riamore was breathless, eyes wide and skin clammy. He trembled slightly as he spoke. "What promise can you give us that you will not fall to that same darkness, my brother?"

Ax's eyes had shut, all emotion gone from his gaunt face. "Lock me away."

Riamore blinked. "What?"

"Lock me away in this tower. Ward me in so I may never leave. I will use the tower to monitor the lands, to cast as much magick as I can to shield them from danger." He opened one eye. "Will that please you, brother?"

Riamore's mouth opened slightly, dumbfounded. "You would rot away alone in here, rather than live out eternity with your bloodlings?"

"If it means protecting that which I love? Yes."

Silence fell once more. Riamore could see there was no use, no sense in standing and wasting air on the argument. "If that is what you wish, Axoliphim."

Ax gave a sigh of exhaustion, sinking lower into his chair. "Yes. It is all I wish. Return that to the others who were too afraid to come here today."

Riamore raised his chin at the insult, turning to stride from the room. He stopped in the doorway, turning to look over his shoulder. "I shall miss you dearly."

Ax was quiet for a moment. "And I you."

And then Riamore was gone.

THE FOLLOWING DAY, only a few short hours before the exodus from Zenafrost, the Zenoths gathered at the Library of Time. They surrounded it in a great circle, joining hands as they began to chant. Axoliphim stood in the threshold of the tower, feeling the wards raise around him. He tested the spell as it grew, finding that no part of him could pass through the threshold of the tower. He could no longer hear his bloodlings chant, barely able to see them through the haze of insurmountable magick.

It was odd, Ax thought as he turned to walk back into the library, how he felt no sadness at this. But instead, a great sense of peace. The tower was able to draw from the earth, as well as give to her. From his spot here within these walls, he would be able to safeguard that which he held most dear. It was all he had left, of Bardro, of Nora, of Ingard, and of his Velisa. Tears welled in his eyes, as they did every time he even thought her name. He shook them off, taking a deep breath and frowning around at the chaos he had wrought in his weeks of misery.

There would be time to mourn later. Eternity was, after all, a very long time.

CHAPTER 12

BARDRO'S BESTIARY

The following are excerpts from the field journal of Bardro, as transcribed by his apprentice, Kivion.

CHAPTER 13
ORB LIGHTS

One of the first things I studied upon our arrival. On first glance, they seemed to merely be tufts of fluorescent plant fibers descending from the rich wildlife all around. But closer inspection has proved this false. Zenafrost is powered by a system of magick flows, webbing underneath the whole of the planet. These veins often expel magickal overflow to the surface, resulting in tiny concentrations of power that take the form of glowing, multi-colored orbs. What is most fascinating, however, is not their creation, but rather their composition. After extensive study, I found that these orbs carry an energy of consciousness. Just as we are watching them, they are watching us. For what, if any, purpose still remains to be seen.

CHAPTER 14
FURIES

One of the more aggressive creatures I have encountered, and the only to present me with a whole-hearted challenge. I have only had the opportunity to find two on my travels, though I am certain there are many more subspecies yet to be discovered. The first I came upon just outside the southern forests. It stood as tall as a mountain, made entirely of stone and earth. I could feel the magick at its core, and it mirrored that of the strange energy below Zenafrost's surface. I have a theory that they are born from the earth itself, but this will require more study. This beast of rock turned to me with eyes that saw everything and nothing. It charged at me with blind rage, unfazed when I fired a warning bolt at its feet. The battle that followed carved blasts of magick and ruin into the surrounding area. Furies seem to absorb most magick, making offensive and defensive strikes exhaustingly difficult. It took a decent amount of my power to best it, and sadly it was destroyed in the process. The same can be said of the second fury, whom I met in the ice-capped tundra to the north. It fought with unending resolve, unrelenting all the way up to its demise. I have several impressive scars from this battle, as the fury harnessed a type of ice magick that caught me wildly off guard.

Strongly suggest avoiding at all costs, as they are nearly impossible to defeat.

CHAPTER 15
BOGDUNOLS

Annoying little bastards. They exist only in the wetlands by the western forest. The mists there are thick and difficult to navigate, even for one as trained as myself. After walking for several hours, I began to hear noises all around me. Footsteps, voices, laughter; always heralded by the very distant sound of bells. The more I ignored this, the closer the noises became. I cleared the area surrounding me with a blast of magick, dissipating the mists momentarily. In this moment, I saw no less than twenty small creatures surrounding me. I would have thought them to be clouds of smoke, could I not see their large green eyes fixated on my face. I sensed no ill intent and attempted to shoo them off. This, however, was a mistake. Far from leaving me in peace, the creatures began to mimic my voice as they followed even more closely through the mists. If I shouted, "Off with you!" fifty more of my voice would echo it back in a near endless chorus. Once they were taught a new word, they would repeat it again and again, as deafening as it was irritating, and yes, all while still following me through those damned, eternal mists. I lost track of the hours I spent lost in those wetlands, berated by my own voice as these creatures ran about underfoot. I would rather walk a whole month, all the way around the forested hills, then ever enter that place again.

A NOTE on the ocean surrounding Zenafrost,

I sense a tremendous magick, far into the depths of the waters by the Western shores. It seems to emanate from everywhere at once, and I cannot place where it originates. I spent two whole nights performing the usual tests, but still naught emerges from the thrashing mess. Will require further research on my next expedition.

A note on the ocean surrounding Zenafrost,

I sense a tremendous magick, far into the depths of the waters by the Western shores. It seems to emanate from everywhere at once, and I cannot place where it originates. I spent two whole nights performing the usual tests, but still naught emerges from the thrashing mess. Will require further research on my next expedition.

CHAPTER 16
BRISËN

After months of careful study and countless hours of devotion to the cause, I had come up with no answer to the mysterious power exuding from the ocean. In a last effort to remedy this (and to quiet my restless mind), I set up camp for myself on the far eastern shores of the continent. I sat there in the white sands for weeks on end, sometimes in silent watch, sometimes experimenting with the ripping tide. I sent all manner of magick into its depths, even going so far as to swim out into its thrashing maw. But the current of the water is untamable, unmanageable. Its impossible strength, stopping even **my** *magick from penetrating its depths, only served to further my frustrations.*

I had all but given up hope for an answer, doomed to my despair that perhaps this would be the first time in all my eternity that I would be left to wonder. It was in this moment that the sand beneath me began to tremble with such ferocity that it began to leap into the air all around. The ocean opened wide in the middle, making a great canyon that the tide dipped waterfalls through. The energy was almighty and overwhelming, and I found myself entirely rooted to my patch of shore. A figure rose from the impossible hole created beyond.

The ocean had come to life to create this magnificent thing. She took the shape of a woman, a woman made entirely of water. It flowed in curves to form her, from supple lips to graceful fingertip. She was surely a terrifying thing, as much as she was beautiful. Eyes like rays of sunlight cast beneath waves of lashes, liquid hair shimmering in the dawn of the horizon. There was a glowing star where her heart would have been, completely hidden were it not for my trained eyes.

I am not ashamed to say that I fell in love in this moment. I dare anyone that is graced with her presence to not, in an instant, submit fully to that which took me.

I fell to my knees in the sand, in reverence and praise. "What are you?" is all I could muster my damned lips to say, so awestruck was I.

"I am the ruler of the tide," she said, in a voice that caressed my ears and drowned me further in the depths of unquestionable yearning. "Wrought from magick and a fallen star, I was created to carry the ocean by the All Mother."

"All Mother..." I said, dazed still by her presence. "Forgive me my arrogance, for I know not of whom you speak."

She bowed her head to me and began to glide closer across the suddenly still surface of the ocean. "You know her by a different name. She is the one that gives all, to all. Your people call her Zenafrost."

It was this that drew me, finally, from my breathlessness. I remember the feeling of shock, the warmth of the sand under my knees taking on new meaning. "Zenafrost...Zenafrost is alive?!"

The goddess of the ocean nodded slowly, nearly level with me now. "Yes. But the All Mother suspects this is something you already knew."

And she was right.

Ever since we had created this planet, ever since we had first stepped foot on its soil...I've known in my heart it was different. Not just in the life we created upon it, but in the life that seemed to exude from ***within*** *it. All the unanswered questions I've penned in this journal, every strange moment and feeling of being watched...it all boiled down to this new truth.*

The woman had come to stand on the edge of the shore, and to my heart-stuttering shock, she too came to kneel before me. She took my hands in hers, and though I felt the instant lick of the ocean across my skin, I felt how solid she was too. For the first time in my life, I desired to hold another; to press them against my body and take her lips in mine as she consumed all I was. And it left me quite breathless as she spoke her next words.

"The All Mother has sent me to you, Bardro. She has seen you walk the world, and the respect you have for all creations she has risen upon it. The ***care*** *you have." She lowered her voice, her ethereal face impossibly close to mine. The sound of my name from her lips, coupled with this closeness, forced me to draw on every ounce of control I could muster.*

"It is this care that has made her entrust this message to you." Her muted tone was filled with an urgency that set all other feeling aside. I would do anything to help her; anything she asked of me. And I told her as such.

"I will do anything. You need only ask it."

Her lashes fluttered, but she continued. "There is a great darkness that has begun to grow in Zenafrost. This force is a terrible thing, and one that could change the course of all our fates. It will drain the All Mother of her magick, drain your kin and kith of theirs. And once it has drawn the life from each and everything that calls this place theirs, it will set forth to destroy all that is pure and good in the cosmos." Her hand came to rest on my cheek, cooling the heat that had risen with her appearance. "You must find this darkness, stop it from its path of imminent destruction. Before destiny is undone forever."

Rage filled me in an instant. Darkness? Come to destroy the home we worked so desperately for; the home that ***Nora*** *had craved since her very creation?*

I placed my hand atop hers on my cheek, holding her stellar gaze as I felt the rush of water beneath my palm. "I give you my word, you and Zenafrost both...tell your All Mother that I will end this plight before her fears come to pass. I will end this threat to our home."

The woman gave me a smile that was made of cosmic dust itself, glinting like the reflection of stars across the ocean's surface on a clear night. "I know you will, Bardro. The All Mother has seen what you hold in your heart. As have I."

The water that built her had grown warm, matching the temperature of my skin as we knelt in watchful silence of one another.

"Please. You must tell me your name," I asked, for how could I ever hope to continue on without knowing what to call my heart.

The woman smiled once more, and from the look on her sculpted face, I'm sure she could have blushed. "Brisën," she said, like music to my soul. "The All Mother calls me Brisën."

Blessed be the Beyonds. I tell you now, this name is what gave me purpose. All I have done, all I am and ever will be, has brought me to this. I knew of love. But she is more than love, in a way I cannot possibly hope to describe in words. I will cry her name from every mountain, every vale; I shall climb the tallest trees in the Forests of Galion and shout it so that all creatures across this world can hear.

As I search for this darkness that scratches at the doorway to our home, to end this dire warning that threatens us all, I do so (however selfishly), for her.

CHAPTER 17
VIKEFO

Though I have known our earth-born friends but a short time, one thing has become abundantly clear: their yearning for growth and knowledge rivals even my own. I say this first to hopefully grant you some small form of understanding for what they've done.

The Forest Dwellers magicks are a mystery, even to them. It seems as though Zenafrost gave them life, gave them purpose, but granted them no explanation on how to wield their mighty gifts. Due to this, the Dwellers have begun experimenting with their magicks in order to better understand what they are capable of. Their cores deal in what can only be described as 'elemental magicks.' The Forest Dwellers are able to not only manipulate the lands they walk upon but conjure forms of earth from seeming nothingness on a whim. Stone, dirt, root, vine...all bow before their powers. It is an incredible sight to behold. And a terrifying one.

As they learn control, mishaps have unfortunately occurred. One of the newer born Dwellers attempted to harness control of the winds nary a month past. For a moment during the ritual, it looked as though he might achieve it. But then we watched as he was suddenly, violently, torn apart before our very eyes. The Elders decreed the winds were to never be sought after again. I have witnessed young Dwellers strangled by vines of their own creation, grown too powerful for them to control. The forest where they are born has become a place unfit for simpler beings to tread. Monsters roam, malformed creatures risen from explosive experimental catastrophes within the woods, creatures like the one I will warn you about here:

The Dwellers wondered if, perhaps, it was possible to combine plant and animal with their magicks. To create something new and wonderful that more closely resembled their image. For what reason they dared act upon such flawed curiosity, I do not know. But act they did. And life indeed sprung forth from this combination of earth magick and plain wolf. Its fur turned green like crawling ivy, veined in glowing stripes of purple poison. Its teeth dripped with moss-colored ooze that ate away at the dirt below and scorched deep into the earth. Whip-like tendrils broke through the flesh on its back, flailing with poison tipped barbs that sought only to kill. Any life-like quality left its eyes, replaced by an eerie, pulsating purple light. This 'Vikefo' as I have dubbed the beast, lunged at all present, managing to strike one of the Dwellers in the process. It fled into the woods, still now hiding away in the twisting shadows of the trees.

The Forest Dweller who was struck by the poisonous monstrosity fell immediately ill and had passed on only a few short days after the event. Since this occurrence, the Forest Dwellers have concocted an antidote to heal most Vikefo wounds, as they have been unable to apprehend their damned creation as of this entry.

CHAPTER 18

WANDERING BARKEN

Yet another instance of strange Forest Dweller magicks.

I'm told they originated from a Forest Dweller barely three weeks of age. Particularly advanced, and uncharacteristically passionate for a Forest Dweller, she had been 'singing and frolicking' through the trees for near a fortnight. She sang songs of the Zenoths creating the world, of the cosmos and the magick that flows through it. She sang of her own birth, and of the things the All Mother had whispered to her before she had drawn breath.

And as she sang and danced and spun, the trees suddenly began to move. They rose up on their roots like feet, joining her in her joyful song and dance. The more she went, the more trees that rose from the dirt to join her. Even when the girl had stopped, the trees continued.

They took off in different directions, singing the tales they had learned, and searching for new tales to tell as they set off. Sometimes the trees they passed would rise alongside them, given the breath of life by whatever magick these 'Wandering Barkens' had been imbued with.

I have witnessed gaggles of them myself on my visits to the Wood. They sing in perfect harmony when together, and it is somewhat impossible to resist joining their jubilant noise when you draw too near. I wonder if this is perhaps another effect of their enchantment. I am interested to see what stories the ones who have begun to travel outside the forests' borders will learn and tell.

CHAPTER 19

A NOTE ON BRISËN

I have been exhausting all efforts in an attempt to narrow down where the darkness is coming from. With Brisën acting as my communication to Zenafrost, we have discovered a few things:

The first dark anomaly came from the bogs towards the Western shores. I was ill surprised by this fact, as I myself had encountered nothing but frustration when passing through those lands (refer to my previous entry on Bogdunols). The world tracks its own magick flows, and after the anomaly originally occurred, it lost all connection to the vein of magick that runs through that area of the world. Brisën has described it to me as a 'large, gaping hole,' void of all feeling, save for dark energy. As our convergence in the Chamber of the Sun *draws near, I shall be setting off immediately to investigate this shadow.*

I admit, my time spent investigating this threat has had a two-fold effect. True, I strive to end the darkness plaguing our home. But I would be a fool and traitor to my heart to say it does not bring me unending joy to spend this time alongside Brisën.

Though she serves as the voice of Zenafrost, she is a creature all her own. Brilliant, powerful, wise...I learn from her every day; I grow from her guidance, and from her love. Perhaps when all this is over, when we have come together to successfully rid ourselves of this looming darkness, I shall give up my eternal quest for knowledge. I never thought it possible, but I have finally found the sort of devotion Nora always spoke of. More than devotion. Cosmic, unending love. It burns the fire within me, to discover this corruption, ever the brighter.

All three of the following accounts took place on the island now known as Hope.

CHAPTER 20

DRAGONS

I encountered these creatures once before, on a world far beyond the cosmos we now reside within. They are ancient beings, perhaps older than even myself, and made of magick well beyond my grasp and understanding. The one I stumbled upon has fallen through the strange rift on the island far into the Brisënbane. The creature was injured, a gaping hole of a wound in its left wing. As I approached, it barred its teeth at me and spat fire molten rock at my feet. "Mind your path, starling," it said to me. "I may be bound to the earth, but my magick is still mightier than yours." I assured the dragon that I meant no harm. Quite the contrary, I took it upon myself to heal the creature to the best that my abilities would allow. Unfortunately for the dragon, their hides are fused with magick, and therefore quite resistant to it. I was only able to patch the wound haphazardly, disallowing for the dragon to rise past cloud level when it took flight. Regardless, the beast was grateful to me. "I owe you a grave favor," it said. "Take one of my scales and carry it with you. One day, when your need is great, I will know to come to your aid." And the aid of a dragon would be quite the sight indeed. So, pluck a scale I did, right from its glimmering red chest. It sits in my breast pocket now as I write this and emits an intense warmth that seems constant.

CHAPTER 21
CONSUMING SHADOWS

This is a creature I never wish to encounter again. It was late in the night, under the light of a red and golden moon. I had just crossed into an area of the island that seemed darker than all the others, as if the full moon's rays did not dare touch the air here. Though the trees were dense, I heard no wildlife alive in the heavy foliage. It was desperately, eerily silent. I did not hear the creature approach, and I am still now unsure if they make any noise at all. I sensed it mere moments before it swept down upon me. I rolled below it as some sort of intelligent shadow dove at my head. Some part of it struck my cheek, tearing the flesh away as if it were made of the lightest silk. It had been so long since blood had been drawn from me, I had almost forgotten what it felt like. I was forced to engage in fight AND flight with this monster. It consumed all magick I threw its way. Even my most powerful abilities disappeared into its shadowed depths. For near an hour, I scrambled tooth and nail to defeat the beast, to no avail. It hunted without feeling, without anything but hunger and cruel intent. It drew so much blood from me, that I feared I would be brought to kneel before it. Just when I thought all was lost, I stumbled from the darkened woods and into an area bathed in moonlight.

I fell through the forest line and into the silvery rays, turning to find the shadow still inches from me. But seemingly unable to pass beyond the borders of its woods. I did not stay to see if the silent killer would vanish with daylight, but I do know that it watched me until I was well out of sight of the forest.

CHAPTER 22

CHANGELINGS

APPROACH WITH EXTREME CAUTION.

I came across this creature on the north shores of the island, sitting in the white sands and watching the tide. It seemed to be covered in some shroud of haze, making it impossible to distinguish in detail from afar. But as I drew closer, the being's shape began to change. It morphed into an exact replica of my brother, Ax, when he was but a newborn starling. The child looked up as I approached, grinning at me. It...it knew things that could have only been obtained through the use of telepathy. And a very advanced form, at that. In my baby brother's voice, it asked me what it was I sought. What it was I truly desired. I could feel some kind of magick pull in my heart when it asked, urging me to answer. And it was this very feeling that made me hold my tongue. The creature promised all my wildest dreams, everything I had ever wanted. But its smile kept stretching, far beyond where it should have been allowed. I could sense ulterior motives. Evil ones. I shook my head and backed away from the creature, with an enormous amount of effort. Were I anyone else, I doubt very much if I would have been able to resist its requests. Even now, I can hear its voice clear as day in my head. Like some horrible itch that can never be scratched. It keeps me up into the night, threatening to drive me mad: "You will come back. They all do, in the end."

CHAPTER 23
THE NECROMANCER

Never in all my years did I imagine I would have to write such an entry as this. My brother...Mezilmoth has been lost. He has fallen to a corrupting shadow that I cannot save him from. My brother, the one I idolized. My brother, the one whose words helped shape the very fabric of all I am. My brother...

I have heard the Fae calling him 'The Deceiver.' And perhaps this is a more suitable title. To call him by his name in these acts of evil tears at my heart in ways I did not know possible. For surely my brother would never do that which I am about to describe.

After the destruction of the Chamber of the Sun, we returned to Zenafrost in search of the Deceiver. But without the Great Crystal to fuel us, we found that our powers had already begun to wane. We tried fruitlessly to track the Deceiver but found only that Zenafrost had been shrouded in a cloud of darkness. This made it impossible to pinpoint his location, as we felt the evil coming from all around us, all at once. We had to rely, in large, on rumor from the Fae villages as the corruption spread. The worst of such rumors have since been confirmed, at the cost of three Zenoth lives.

In a village hidden within the forests to the East, there lived a Fae who had learned the art of healing. His magick lent itself to the earth, and the Dwellers in the woods agreed to help him hone his ability into the unique craft he became known for. He was the paragon of his village, drawing Fae and Zenoth alike to garner aid from his healing gifts. This gift made him a target for the Deceiver, and it was not long before the dark shadow of Mezilmoth came to the woods. I am told the Fae Healer denied Mezilmoth's wishes, denied him the request of joining his growing army. The Fae and his villagers rose as one, combining their magicks into a great shield that surrounded their home. It was a valiant effort.

But it was not enough.

I have heard many versions of the events that followed. From these fragmented pieces of nightmarish tales, we have been able to string together what we believe occurred. The Deceiver destroyed their great shield in one fell swoop. He set their village ablaze, forcing the Fae from their homes like cattle, trapped in wait for death. One by one, Mezilmoth tore the villagers apart. TORE THEM APART. He extracted their magick cores from their souls, and consumed their powers whole as he went. None of their magick could stop him, and they were forced to watch as their friends, their families, their loved ones...all perished before him. The healer begged him to stop, pledged his obedience to the dark tide if he would just spare the others. But his cries fell on deaf ears. Finally, it was only the healer left alive before the Deceiver. And it was then that Mezilmoth offered him a solution: "Join me, and you will have the power to bring them all back. To raise all I have ended and give them life once more."

And in his blind agony, the healer agreed.

Just as we gifted parts of our magick cores to the Fae, so did Mezilmoth imbue his darkness with the healer. The corruption...it changed him into a monster. His skin fell away, his insides twisting around the bone in great stretches of pulsating muscle. His blood turned black, his magick grew dark. I am told that his screams echoed all the way to the northern shores; that he ripped his face away from the bone with his bare fingers. And Mezilmoth kept to his word, in a fashion. The healer was given the ability to raise the dead. But it was not life that he gave them. Their bodies rose from the earth in the same manner in which they had fallen: Bloodied, torn apart, pieced together only by root, rock and corrupted magicks. They had no souls, no thoughts of their own. They served only the Deceiver, just as the fallen healer now did. An army of the damned, ready for a battle where it would be impossible to stop them. For how does one kill that which is already dead?

The healer is now known only as 'The Necromancer.' We classify him as a 'Prime Corruption,' a being of such horrific magick, that only the power of the Zenoths stand a chance of keeping him at bay. And barely, at that. I have lost three of my kin to this specific monster in the last few years alone. As my brother...as the Deceiver continues to ravage the lands, he consumes the magick cores of all he encounters. A terrible death. And from his shadow, the Necromancer then comes to raise these dead as mindless soldiers. They number in the thousands now and must be reduced to dust in order to stop them completely.

I fear that this is only the beginning of whatever dark plans Mezilmoth has in store for the Fae, for Zenafrost, and for ALL of the cosmos.

FABLES AND LEGENDS

CHAPTER 24

THE LEGEND OF THE TIE

Once upon a time, there were the Zenoths and the Fae they had created. The Zenoths so loved these beings they had birthed into the world, that they chose to give them a tremendous gift: the blessing of their magick.

Each Zenoth split their power, the energy then seeking the two Fae it was most compatible with. It would fuse with their souls, creating something new entirely. These Fae that shared a magick core were drawn to one another, bound by the threads of fate as their magicks fought to become whole once more. These Tied users were able to harness a combined power that rivaled even the mightiest of Zenoths. It was an incredible force, more magnificent than any in the cosmos. The souls of the users would cry out to one another, no matter the distance, forging an unbreakable bond that surpassed the bonds of time itself.

During the great Exodus, this bond was severely shaken. The magick wavered as the Zenoths and many of the Fae abandoned Zenafrost for untainted lands. Through the ages, the bloodlines that held these original cores became more and more diluted. Eventually, this led to the Tied users dying out entirely, the remaining magicks but a shade of what once was.

CHAPTER 25
THE DRAGON PRIESTESS

Once upon a time, there lived a woman whose bloodline had been tainted with dark magicks. This corrupted the core power inside of them, creating monsters of their men and women.

Their family name was Tylwyth, and the woman born of this lineage was Caerani. She was the last child of the Tylwyths, born just before her parents were each destroyed by their own dark magick. She raised herself, learning very young how cruel her curse truly was. Untamed and unmanageable, this darkness would explode from her in great bursts of destruction, leaving nothing but death and ruin in her wake.

Such was the case of the village in the mountains. Caerani was still only a child but had managed to keep her magick contained for nearly two years. Then came the Druidian War, and the invasion thereafter. They came to the village, came to burn it down with all inside. And Caerani tried with all her might to harness this darkness within her; harness it and destroy the enemy.

But her power was too great, and she smote all life and remnants of the village from the earth in mere seconds.

Heartbroken, condemned to a life of agony due to her cursed magick, the child Tylwyth roamed the vast expanse of Zenafrost. Alone, adrift. She walked for days, weeks, months, never stopping; always staying far from any sign of other life. Her feet were bloodied, and her body frail when she came to the eastern shores of Zenafrost. Here, Caerani fell to her knees in the white sands. And here she wept, her tears joining with the rushing tide of the ocean.

As she cried, there came a sound like thunder from above. Great gusts of wind blew sand in torrents around her, whipping her head down to shield her face. The shore shook, then all fell still.

When she opened her eyes, she found herself knelt before a great red dragon. His golden eyes were fixated on her from high above, the sun framed betwixt his horns. His wings sat furled against his body, glinting like diamonds in their glory. He sat, digging massive talons into the soft sand.

"Why is it you weep, daughter of Fae?" he asked, but Caerani could feel the dark magick building within her from the fear she felt.

"You must leave!" the youngling cried, scrambling to her feet and rushing backwards across the sand. "Take to the skies, as high as you can fly! I cannot control it! Please-!"

But the dragon did not move.

Caerani screamed, the overwhelming intensity of her power racing from her body. With a *boom* that shook both land and sea, dark magick erupted forth. It blasted a great crater in the shoreline, the ocean fleeing from its might before it pooled into this fresh crevasse. Caerani fell to her knees in the tide, broken and beaten. She stared through the dust created from the explosion, searching for the remains of the dragon.

"Ah. It was this power that called forth to me then," The dragon stood unscathed, brushing sand from his great shoulders as if nothing had happened. Caerani stared in astonishment.

"But...but how is this possible?" she asked, scarcely allowing herself to believe it. "Nothing ever survives those outbursts. *Nothing*."

"*I* am not nothing, child," the dragon replied. "Your magick has called to me. Begged I help return it, and you, to the light. Is that not what you wish?"

"I wish to no longer be," Caerani whispered in return, tears streaming from her eyes. "I cannot bear the things I have done."

The dragon's uncompromising gaze softened as he replied. "You are not responsible for the evils brought by your blood. But if you insist on atoning for your so-called sins, then come with me. I will heal your core, and we shall work as one to restore your soul with it."

The dragon bowed low, exposing his back to Caerani in offering. She stood, too stunned to speak. And as if of their own accord, pulled forth perhaps by the strings of destiny, her feet drew her to the dragon's side. She used her final strength to pull herself atop the dragon's scaled spine. Her thin arms hugged as tight as they could round its neck, and with a great beat of his wings, they were off.

The dragon carried the child to his home upon the isle now called Hope. It is here Caerani's darkness was rent from her core, from the very fabric of the cursed bloodline she was born to. In exchange for the gap it left behind, the dragon gave upon Caerani Tylwyth a gift matching that of the Zenoths to the Fae: a piece of their own core.

From this selfless act, the first fire user was born; raised from the ashes of her despair and trained by dragons to wield its might. Legend states Caerani is the only one who harnesses this ability, in all the history of Zenafrost.

CHAPTER 26
YVONAR OF THE ACCURSED MOON

Once upon a time, there stood a village hidden within a great wood. This village hosted the royal court of the Odelians and was protected by the brunt of their military might. The Odelian Warriors, renowned for their prowess in magick, had set up the village as their home. Training fields littered the outer-reaches of the forest line, while taverns and weapons and armor-smiths made their home in the village beyond. Hopefuls vied for their chance to partake in the legendary Trials, the only way they could progress to becoming a true Odelian Warrior.

Yvonar was only a youngling when he first began his training. His bloodline's magick had begun to dwindle with the years, one of the many whose powers had become diminished with the darkening of the lands. On his first run of the Trials, Yvonar failed in the very first task. The healer had said he was lucky to be alive, with how much blood he had lost in the woods. Runs two, three and four of the Trials, he had completed the first task only to be torn asunder by the horrors of the second. It had taken him near a month to recover with each failure. On his final loss, General Lightcleaver had barred him from the training fields, barred him from the Trials, barred him from ever being a Warrior.

Yvonar was heartbroken, enraged at his own incapability. He watched as all his friends either failed in their Trials, died trying to complete them, or rose victorious at the end. Those who were lucky enough to do so were assigned to War Parties and dispatched off into Zenafrost, to seldom be seen again.

On the eve before the full moon one balmy fall night, the great King Leionas called for a meeting of all in the Hidden Village. Yvonar sat near the back of the crowd, watching as the King took to the podium with his Honor Guard: Drake, with his confident swagger and plentiful blades; Caerani, the fabled fire user who was rumored to truly be part dragon; and the Princess. Alora. Yvonar couldn't bear to look at her for long, too overwhelmed by her beauty and the things she made him feel. He was glad when Drake began to speak, pulling their attention.

"A creature slipped from the rift on the island of Hope," he said. "It bit one of my men in the battle that followed, unbeknownst to any of us at the time." His expression was dark. "Though the creature itself is now dead, we have reason to believe my man was tainted by it. Turned by it." His words were met with a wave of hushed whispers.

Caerani raised a hand, silencing them before she spoke. "This man is becoming the ruthless monster that emerged from the rift and attacked us one month ago tomorrow. Upon our arrival back in port, he took off into the forest before we could detain him."

"We're in danger, then?" cried the weaponsmith, Delphine Gofannon. She clutched her child close to her bosom, squeezing him in panic despite his protests.

"We are in no danger," Alora replied calmly. Her voice was like warm sunshine in Yvonar's heart. "We mean only to keep you informed. And to ask you to stay in your homes until the man can be caught." She nodded towards General Lightcleaver, standing on the edge of the podium and surrounded by the Odelian War Parties.

"The General and his comrades will follow us into the forest tonight. We'll sort it out in no time."

The General inclined his head in a slight bow to Alora, the Warriors behind him dropping to their knees in respect before they turned and departed.

Yvonar was struck by a sudden idea. If he could help capture the beast, perhaps he could win the General's favor and be granted the chance to rejoin the Hopefuls once more. He stood from his seat as the crowd dispersed, resolved to his decision.

YVONAR WALKED ALONE through the forest, nearly four hours after their departure. The General had laughed at his request to join them, commanding he stay put and "help the commonfolk hide." Yvonar had grown enraged at this, determined then to set out on his own. If the General would not have him, then he would best the beast himself to prove his worth.

The sounds of nightlife around him had quieted as he walked, and he drew his battleaxe with no time to spare. From the shadows of the trees, something sprung at him. Yvonar dove out of the way, spinning around the see the massive form gathering itself from the place he had just stood. It looked like a wolf of some sort, but Yvonar had never seen a wolf or dog of any sort the size of this thing. It turned to face him, and Yvonar's blood ran cold.

He was twelve feet tall, covered from head to foot in thick black fur. He stood on two legs, the elongated paws ending in blood-stained claws that dug into the dirt below. His jaws were open, drooling thick, red liquid and revealing a mouth full of sharp fangs. Yvonar could see bits of freshly ripped flesh caught between them. His eyes were the color of bone, his fingers stretched into pointed tips that could have been daggers, they were so sharp. And Yvonar might have been able to convince himself this was some sort of corrupted wolf, had it not been for the bits of torn clothing still clinging from his arms and legs. This was no wolf.

It was the member of Drake's crew who had been bitten.

Yvonar watched as he threw his shaggy head back and let out a bloodcurdling howl. Gritting his teeth, he tightened the grip on his battle axe and roared back. The creature lunged again. Yvonar was ready this time. He swung the axe high overhead. The beast dodged, the axe glancing off his hide. His claws grazed Yvonar's shoulder, drawing blood. Yvonar swung again. This time, the force was met with the wet drive of blade through flesh. The monster roared, and before Yvonar could finish the fatal blow of his weapon, the beast latched its jaws onto Yvonar's bicep.

Yvonar cried out in pain and triumph, the beast cleaving nearly in two as his axe set to work. The jaw remained locked; the teeth sunk deep into Yvonar's arm. He dropped his axe, wrenching open the dead beast's mouth and freeing himself. His bicep was bleeding profusely, perfectly shaped teeth marks driven far into the muscle. His heart gave an odd shudder, and a cold wave washed over him.

If this man had been transformed by the Rift Beast biting him, it only stood to reason that the same was now happening to Yvonar. His pulse pounded in his ears, thinking of the Odelian War Parties now scouring the woods, searching for a beast like the one he was about to become. Then his mind drifted to Alora; beautiful, sweet Alora who always looked at him with such caring eyes...

He could not stand the idea of putting her in harm's way.

Steadfast to his new mission, Yvonar shouldered his bloody battle axe and took off deeper into the woods. If he could get beyond the border of the Forgotten Wood, he would pass into the territory of the ancient Druids. Like the monster who had started this curse, the Druids had emerged long ago from the rift on the island called Hope. They worshipped a Moon God, one from a land far beyond Zenafrost or the cosmos surrounding. The Druids had been chased from their world by invaders, making their court here in the Forests of Galion. The Odelian Warriors knew better than to pass beyond their borders, or risk incurring the wrath of the Druids. But Yvonar had no choice. He had to keep his people, his love, safe.

So off he set into the woods, feeling the itch of change within him with every passing step. It took him hours, well beyond the rise of the sun, to reach the borders. There was a wall of throned bramble that stretched from deep into the earth to well past the canopy of trees above. It wove between trees, creating an impassible barrier, save for one unseemly looking gate wrought into the very bottom. It was made of root and vine, hanging open on its hinges in mock welcome.

Yvonar was feeling a strange rage growing in the pit of his stomach. It was like nothing he had ever felt before, setting his teeth on edge and pulse racing. The uncomfortable shift in energy as he passed through the gate only served to double this sensation, until he was quite sure he would kill the first thing he came across.

As if in response to this, there was movement from the treetops above. Yvonar swung his bare hands at whatever swept down behind him. By the time he had spun around to face it, the figure was gone. He could smell it in the air, feel its strange magick energy stifling the air.

"Well. That's a mighty awful curse you've got there, wildling."

Yvonar spun around, eyes wild, expecting to see a man standing behind him. But instead, he found a man suspended high in the air.

He was upside-down, tendrils of grey hair hanging around his dark skin. His head was tilted, curiosity lacing a pair of completely white eyes. He was wearing clothes made of what looked like sewn-together leaves. "A fresh one too, at that," he added to his first statement.

Yvonar leapt backwards, unsheathing his battle axe and snarling at the man like a wounded beast. "Be gone, Druid! I cannot control what is to come!"

The Druid righted himself in the air, coming to sit with his head still cocked at Yvonar. "No, I doubt very much if anyone can rightly control a mark from the Accursed Moon."

Yvonar blinked, momentarily distracted by the phrase. "The Accursed...what?"

The Druid motioned towards Yvonar's bicep, and he looked to his wound.

It had healed completely, leaving what looked like deep runic markings scarred red into his flesh. Yvonar's eyes widened as he stared.

"That sort of mark does not exist in this world," The Druid went on. "Where did you get such a thing, friend?"

Yvonar scowled, once again feeling the overwhelming need to attack, to throw himself at the Druid and tear out his throat. "The rift. A beast brought it with him through the rift."

"Ah," the Druid said, descending to the ground before Yvonar. "And right on the eve of the Full Moon. Incredibly poor luck on your part."

Yvonar tightened his grip on his battle axe and spoke through his teeth. "Leave here or I will tear you apart limb by limb. I. Cannot. Control. It." He emphasized each word clearly.

The Druid's eyes narrowed. "You should have transformed already. You're putting up a valiant fight against the curse." He looked thoughtful for a moment. "Perhaps...perhaps, I may be of help to you. I can sense something in you, wildling. It smells of destiny and fate." He gave Yvonar a wide grin. "And I do so love to interject myself into the workings of the Gods' greater plans."

Yvonar felt like he was about to burst into flame. He was trembling from head to toe from forced control. He roared at the Druid, "RUN, you FOOL!" and raised the battle axe high, trying with all his might to stop himself.

The Druid was raising his arms as well, pointing them towards the darkening sky beyond the canopy. Suddenly, they were bathed in tremendous moonlight. The Druid was chanting something in a foreign tongue, his white eyes glowing.

Yvonar was being pulled into the air, his limbs freezing like stone. He was cold as ice, his heartbeat becoming the only sound in his ears.

The Druid had risen into the air before him, eyes glowing like the moonlight that shrouded them. He raised his hand, placing it against the broadside of Yvonar's battle axe. He did not speak, but a voice resounded inside Yvonar's head.

"Accursed One, I see your heart. The purity in your soul fights for salvation, and I will heed its cry. I bind you by the power of the Moon God, Lleuad. I bathe your magick in the light of the Celestial and shed you of the darkness that has rotted your kin."

The battle axe began to vibrate, the metal changing before their very eyes. It morphed from black to pale blue, white runes etching up the hilt. The runes stretched off the metal, burning onto Yvonar's skin as they worked their way up, up, up. They did not stop until they had reached the wound left by the beast, covering the red markings in their fiery, white light.

The voice sounded in his head once more. "You will be moonlight's reckoning. The justice from the shadows of this land. You are Lleuad's sword and shield. Your destiny is one bound with all, son of old. Now, you must rise to the occasion."

Yvonar remained here in the Forests of Galion for 30 years, before his return to the Hidden Village. Legend states that his weapon was 'the arm of a God itself,' rivaled only by the power he melded with it. On the King's decree, he entered the Trials and emerged the only successful one of his group. He never joined a War Party, for fear that one day the wards that sealed his curse would break in combat, releasing the monster within. Single-handedly, Yvonar served as a weapon to the Odelian crown, turning the tide of many battles alongside the King's Honor Guard. It was only upon Alora's stalwart and exasperated confession of returned love for him, that Yvonar allowed himself to be partnered with another.

Yvonar of the Accursed Moon went on to be a great friend and ally to the Druids, the only King to ever maintain a loose allegiance with them during his rule.

Upon his passing, the gate that connected the Forgotten Woods to the Forest of Galion was sealed, and all ties with the Druids and their mystical ways were severed.

CHAPTER 27

THE CAT AND THE CURSE

Once upon a time, there stood a land abandoned by those who created it. The beings left on this doomed world split into factions based on their magick cores, or lack thereof. Those with the least diluted magicks became known as the Odelians. The Odelian people were, for the most part, honorable, steadfast, and resolute in their belief that they could save their world. They took up arms, many becoming great warriors and protectors of Zenafrost. While still others grew mad with their powers, using their magick for selfish, evil endeavors. This was especially true for a young Odelian man by the name of Vinrick.

Vinrick grew up the son of an Odelian War Captain. His magick core was based in mineral magick, giving him control over rock, metal, crystal, and ore. It was during his third Trial to become an Odelian Warrior himself that Vinrick first tasted the sweet poison of power. He stumbled upon a treasure in the crypts below the Hidden Village; a ring left behind by the High Fae that granted him access to the magick flows that stemmed through Zenafrost. This increased Vinrick's magick exponentially. But it was not without a price. The ring took tiny pieces of his soul each time he used it, sapping him of his loves and morals. And with each use, Vinrick cared less and less about the loss.

By the time he was fully a man, Vinrick had left the Hidden Village behind in search of greater power. His goal was to discover how the Fae and Zenoths had left their world all those centuries ago, and to grow mighty enough to follow them. He plundered gravesites, raided temples, killed any who stood in his way, or were unlucky enough to cross his path. All in his pursuit of becoming 'All-Powerful.' He gained many ancient relics during this time, ranging from simple charms that imbued his core with more magick, to the very heart of the ocean itself which he stole from her thrashing depths. He thought himself unstoppable, and perhaps he was. It was this thought that led him to find himself within the halls of the Tower of Wrought Time.

The Tower was a place of myth and legend. A catch-all for things from all dimensions, all worlds; it was dangerous, deadly. Many had entered through its doors in the past, and only a handful had ever reemerged. But Vinrick was cunning, and fearless, and hungry. He found the travelling Tower when it appeared in the Deep Wood, far from the Hidden Village. Its dark hallways seemed to travel on forever, with no ceiling or end in sight. They were filled as high and far as the eye could see with mystical treasures of all kinds. But they were trivial to Vinrick, their power nothing compared to what he sought. He could feel an unyielding magick from somewhere deep within the Tower, and he was making his way for it when he stumbled upon something worth pausing for.

Amidst the mountains of glittering gold and gemstones stood a wooden stand, much like the kinds he had seen at market in the villages. A sign hung from its front, with the words "TOE EMPORIUM" etched into it. A large brown cat sat on a stool behind it, blinking slowly at him with its great, green eyes. The cat had been clothed in a multi-colored cloth vest, by what Vinrick assumed was its absent owner. A bin sat before the cat, filled with all manners of trinkets and charms that were clearly the source of the tremendous power Vinrick was now feeling. There was a bell lying next to the bin, with a small paper sign that read "Ring for Service".

Vinrick let out a dark chuckle, looking around quickly. Whatever fool had left this bin unattended would soon learn the lesson to never do so again. Satisfied that the owner of the stand was nowhere near, Vinrick took the bin in his hands. And suddenly, he found himself unable to move. Even with all his accumulated magicks, he could not fight off whatever had locked him into place with this box.

"Hmm. I wish I could say I was surprised."

Vinrick flicked his eyes upwards, still frozen. He expected to see a man standing there, surely the owner of this stand and the bin of treasures he was now caught red-handed with. But the only thing there was the cat. And he was now standing on his hind legs atop the stool, arms crossed and shaking his head at Vinrick.

"You know, my nose can pick up on greed from a thousand marks away. And I scented you out the moment you entered the Tower." He gestured towards the paper sign beside the bell with a clawed paw. "I saw you read my signs, and yet you chose to steal the bin anyway." He cocked his head, the pupils of his green eyes becoming slits. "Ah. And I see you have stolen a great many things in your time, son of Fae. Your magick...why, I cannot even sense your true core through all of the massacred bits you have collected within you."

The cat whispered words in a language Vinrick did not understand, and the box was suddenly back in its original spot before him. Vinrick remained frozen, hands suspended in place as if they were still holding the box. He could feel his magick cracking through whatever strange hold had been placed on him, urging himself to break out faster.

The cat had returned his attention to Vinrick, sighing. "I can smell blood on you. Men, women, children...all taken in your pursuit of power. I have met many, many like you in my travels, and have seen the destruction that follows in your wake. You have been abandoned by your soul, and I am afraid there is no hope of it returning."

Vinrick had broken through the magick binding him just enough to speak. “You know nothing of me, you pest!” he spat at the cat, baring his teeth. “I have no use for a soul. I desire only magick, and I will wring it from every inch of this damned Tower. Starting with YOU!” He broke a hand free of the bind and raised it high.

But the cat merely raised a finger. Vinrick was entirely frozen once more, and he felt his tongue become fused to the roof of his mouth. The cat continued as if he had never been interrupted. “Typically, I kill men like you. It simplifies the problem, you see. No evildoer, no evil. But you...” He pet his chin, stroking the smooth fur down to a point. “You have quite the magick hoard within you. Enough to power my travels for many, many years to come. Yes...yes, I think that would be most fitting.”

The cat raised its hands, and Vinrick felt like he was being squeezed from all sides. He couldn’t breathe, couldn’t move, couldn’t fight as the cat’s strange voice boomed around him on an unnatural wind. “Vinrick, son of Fae, Collector of Blood and Power. Your life has been spent stealing the lives of others. You laid your own soul as forfeit on this path. And for this, your curse shall be mine to bestow.”

Vinrick felt the squeezing grow tighter, and the world seemed to be growing around him. No, not growing. Vinrick had begun to shrink.

“The stolen magick within you cannot be returned. So instead, it will be used. You will be nothing but a battery, Vinrick, trapped within my Emporium to power my travel to other worlds. You will be aware of it all, feel every bit that is taken back from you. You will watch as everything you took is, in turn, taken from you.”

Vinrick was the size of an orange now, screaming in pain but unable to make a sound. The cat stooped low and scooped the tiny Vinrick from the floor of the Tower. He walked behind the stand and placed the frozen Vinrick in a small slot beneath the counter. The cat grinned down at him, perching atop the wooden stool once more. “Excellent. Let’s get to work then, shall we?”

MAJOR LANDMARKS

CHAPTER 28

DELINVAL

(DELL-IN-VALL)

When the Zenoths gifted their magick unto the Fae of Zenafrost, they presented them first with a choice: change the fate of your bloodline forever, or remain just as you are. Those who took the gift became imbued with a magick core, granted immortality as true equals to the Zenoths. Those who chose not to take the gift evolved much differently as time went on.

They lost the characteristic point to their ears, the vague glowing that emitted from their skin. Their life spans were greatly shortened by comparison, existing only 80 to 90 years before passing on to the Beyonds or the End of All Things. Many set up small villages across the flowing countryside, up in to the Krakenbär Mountains and further. But even more, most especially those who had risen as leaders amongst these once-Fae, gathered together to create a beacon for their peoples.

From the meadows on the westernmost side of the continent, they raised a mighty kingdom. Built from the ocean-stained stone of the cliffsides and adorned in glistening gemstones from their magick-using allies to the east, Delinval became the center of light for all of Zenafrost. In the time before the Great War, once-Fae and magick-users alike gathered to live as one within the white city, overseen by a bloodline as old as the earth itself. Trade flourished and life boomed, all supposedly equal beneath the crown.

After his victory in the Great War, King Grathiel was forced to shut the gates of the kingdom, practically for good. Few but merchants and tradesfolk were allowed in and out of their borders, the king determined to keep his people protected from the darkness spreading beyond. This allowed life to continue springing from the grounds within the white stone walls, leaving it as one of the last strongholds to still bear green flora, fruit, and flower in the whole of Zenafrost. Their filtration system, developed by Grathiel and the craftsman of Delinval, keeps their section of the Endless River purified from the corruption plaguing the lands.

CHAPTER 29

THE FORGOTTEN WOODS

(IN ELDER TONGUE: THE GREEN WOMB)

When the Zenoths first set foot on Zenafrost's soil, they came to stand before a great forest. Stretching across the eastern side of the continent, nearly covering its entirety, the woods were unlike any the Zenoths had built before. Trees that shifted color with the phase of the moon towered towards the skies, morphing from green to red to blue to pink. Others were covered in sharp needles that grew glowing flowers in an instant when dropped to the earth below. Bushes that produced fruit which, when consumed, gave you the ability to speak to animals; some that gave you the ability to commune with the plants. Bird song mixed with the twinkling of bells, though it was impossible to pin down exactly where these chiming noises originated from.

As the centuries passed in Zenafrost and the Fae grew and evolved alongside the Zenoths, so too did the world itself. From this eastern wood sprung forth glowing orbs of light, shifting into every color imaginable along with the trees. They flitted across the corners of Zenafrost, and upon closer observation, seemed to also be studying all that they saw. They held a sentience that even Bardro, the most learned of the Zenoths, could not understand.

Just one year before the start of the cosmic battle that nearly destroyed Zenafrost, a new being rose from this same mysterious forest. They stood as the Fae did, almost identical to the Zenoth's creations in all ways, save for their strangely earthen appearances. They looked to be partially made of plant and flora, of stone and sky. They were born from the very heart of the forest, rising from the dirt as a tree or flower might. The Forest Dwellers referred to Zenafrost as The All Mother, and the woods they called home, The Green Womb. Their magick was that of the earth, controlling root and rock and all things in between. They served Zenafrost, and were the first and last to be created by her strange and sentient magick. Mighty as they were, they were beings of peace; speakers for the one they called All Mother, and steadfast in their stance against conflict on her soils.

As the magick across Zenafrost shifted, the elements beginning to corrupt, the Forest Dwellers warded the borders of the great wood. This ward rivaled even the Zenoth's magicks, shielding it from the damage they knew was to come. None would be allowed passage, without the blessing of the Dwellers and, therefore, Zenafrost herself.

It was this all-powerful ward that kept the woods safe from the corruption that began to poison the world. Even as the darkness ate away the earth that lay around it, nothing came to touch the Forest Dwellers and their home. It came to be known as The Forgotten Woods, a mystery to nearly all throughout the course of history.

Here is where the last of Zenafrost's magick retreated to, the last bit untouched and untainted by the consuming darkness. Purity lives within the shadows of the forest, using every bit of itself to hold the final line against the inevitable.

CHAPTER 30

THE FORESTS OF GALION

(GAL-EE-ON)

In order for the Zenoths to travel the cosmos, they created a portal to the Chamber of the Sun. The Chamber was a hub, connected to all manners of pathways throughout the universe. When the Chamber fell to the darkness, the portal became a rift; a tear in the fabric of reality and all that was. The Zenoths did their best to contain this instability of magick, barricading it on an island guarded by two immortal soldiers of Zenafrost. On rare occasion (such as with the dragons that came to call Zenafrost home), the beings that fell through the rift were impossible to control. They were able to escape the confines of the ever-changing island and reach the mainlands. This was the case for the Druids.

The Druids, beings from a far-off land that worshipped ancient celestial Gods, were forced from their world by an indominable threat. They travelled through a portal in their land, not knowing where it would lead them. When they emerged on the other side, it was to find a world in chaos. Dark magick threatened all that was, the earth they tread upon screamed out in agony as the corruption tore through its core. The Druids, afraid of what this monumental and uncontrolled magick could do to a soul, retreated to a nearly untouched portion of deep wood. This forest, just west of the mountainous borders of the Forgotten Woods, became the new home for the Druids.

A home they were determined to protect at all costs.

With their strange and foreign magick, they drew a great barrier around their portion of forest. It shielded them from any that were tainted by the darkness and set a firm boundary to all others that dared pass its borders. The Druids, led by a magick user named Galion, began to rebuild their lost lives there. Though they respected Zenafrost and the laws that governed it, the Druids served only the Gods from their old world; the Gods that granted them their powers and seemingly eternal life.

The Druids were unfriendly, to put it mildly. They did not take kindly to intruders, punishing those foolish enough to cross into their lands with the utmost severity. Rogue armies have arisen from the mysterious forest in the past, bent on conquering more land for their people. They have yet to be successful, though the battles wrought from their attempts have been those of dark legend and warning.

The only 'child of Zenafrost' to have ever been granted safe passage through the Forests of Galion was Yvonar the Accursed. Under his rule as King of the Odelians, they were able to hold a fragile alliance with the Druids. They assisted in the Great War, aiding in many of its blood fueled battles when it first began. But with the death of King Yvonar at the hands of the darkness, all connections to the Forest and the Druids were lost.

The shields around the Forest have since multiplied, with no word from within for the last twenty years. The only unwarded entrance is a small garden gate, located deep within the Forgotten Woods where the two forests meet. Most Forest Dwellers and Odelians know this not to be an invitation, but a test of wisdom.

All those unwise enough to pass through the gate have suffered the gravest of consequences in return.

CHAPTER 31
YLASTRA
(ILL-AS-TRUH)

When Mezilmoth began his quest to overtake the cosmos, his first step was to test the extent of his dark powers. He took a Fae under his wing, one who had lost his way in the world and sought for a purpose once more. Together, they travelled deep into the marshes to the West. Mezilmoth had dug down into the earth here, blowing massive holes far below the surface in search of Zenafrost's core. He found instead that his powers left the earth blackened, corrupted, and decaying. Darkness seemed to emanate from the deepest of these pits, spawning clouds of corruption and madness.

It is on the edge of this cavernous abyss that Mezilmoth attempted to imbue his found Fae, Normigone, with his magick. He split his magick core in two, just as the Zenoths had done for the Fae so many moons ago. He placed it within Normigone, felt it fuse with his soul.

Then he watched as it drove Normigone mad.

Though the Fae's body proved powerful enough to withstand the change, his soul and the magick already within him became warped.

He spoke of voices in the shadows, calling to him. Begging him to be released. Mezilmoth saw the manic madness become unstoppable within his mind, filling him with a crusade-like drive. It was an insanity that Mezilmoth could not risk hindering his plans. Instead of destroying Normigone, his first failed experiment, he instead chose to lock him away, in case he could be of future use.

In the stone and shadow of the pit he made beneath the bogs, Mezilmoth sealed Normigone away. He would never be able to leave this place but could do as he wished within its confines. And that was the last Mezilmoth the Deceiver saw of Normigone.

Sealed in the dark underbelly of Zenafrost, filled with the dark power of the fallen Zenoth, Normigone listened to the whispering voices that hounded him relentlessly. They spoke to him of divine right, of how he was chosen to be creator and King of a new ring of evolution. Guided by these dark whispers, Normigone used his powers to erect a great kingdom beneath the surface. Built from the stone, born from the black abyss. And when he was finished, it is said that the shadows bore a crown of night onto his head.

"King Normigone," they echoed, "it is time you freed us. Time to bring your children to the kingdom. This kingdom of Ylastra."

It is unknown how, exactly, the rising of the Chaos Users took place. It is widely thought that Normigone used his powers to form shape to the voices that whispered in the shadows. The voices that many think were spawned in the pit of corruption the dark kingdom surrounded. Their skin was dark as the eternal night they lived within, their powers uncontrollable and nigh unstoppable. Some could turn themselves into great beasts, akin to the ferocity of Furies or Dragons. Others could only ever use this transformation once, as they were too weak to reverse it once started. Though Normigone was sealed within the walls of the dark kingdom, his Ylastrians could take to the surface in the shadows of night and storm.

The Chaos Users partook in many wars throughout history, siding with whomever King Normigone commanded them to.

Normigone remains the only being capable of controlling the Chaos Beasts once they are transformed, and many speculate that this is due to his magick's connection to them.

Though Ylastra sided with Delinval in the Great War, they hold no friendships with *any* entities on Zenafrost.

CPSIA information can be obtained
at www.ICGtesting.com
Printed in the USA
LVHW091743150723
752491LV00036B/719

9 798385 750368